WHERE THERE ARE
DRAGONS

AN ANTHOLOGY OF MIXED EMOTIONS

Edited By

James Jakins | Austin James | J.L. Mayne

Stories and Poems By

Dr. Benjamin Anthony | Donald Arfield
Maxwell Bauman | Melanie Bowling | Dani Brown |
Justin A. Burnett | Garrett Cook | Dav Crabes
Ashley Dioses | Fiona Maeve Geist | Bo Hernö
Seth Hunsaker | James Jakins | Austin James
Christopher Lesko | J.L. Mayne | Christine Morgan
Jessica Amanda Salmonson | Eric James Stone

Presented by Robber's Dog Pub

CONTENTS

INTRODUCTION

Firstly, thank you for picking up our book. It's a project we at Robber's Dog Pub are very proud of. A project close to our hearts.

You may have noticed that the book's description states it's an anthology for charity. Proceeds from every sale are going to support Suicide Awareness and Prevention.

It's a cause we believe in. It's one that has touched the lives of everyone at Robber's Dog, as well as many of the writers appearing in this book.

If you'll allow me, I'd like to tell you a little about my friend Daniel.

In February of 2017 he took his own life. He left a vacancy in the world that will never be filled. And, for completely selfish reasons, I still miss him to this day.

He was such an intricate and major part of my life that for a long time I didn't know how to cope without him there, there are still days, two years later, when I have to wonder how I get by without our daily conversations. Without our talks about fantasy novels we've read, or shows we've watched.

We would recommend books and shows and games to each other all the time. I knew that if ever I wanted to get him to move one of my recommendations to the top of his list all I had to do was tell him it had dragons in it.

He loved dragons. And that's where this book's theme came from. We could pretend that it's something bigger, that it's some metaphor about slaying our inner dragons or something like that, but no. It's because my friend Daniel loved dragons and, if I'm being honest, almost every book I've ever released was, at least a little bit, just done to impress him.

I'm sure every one of our writers has someone they'd like to dedicate this book to, so this book is for them. This book is for anyone you've lost. And this book is for Daniel.

- James Jakins
Robber's Dog Pub

ACCOUNTING FOR DRAGONS

BY ERIC JAMES STONE

Introduction

Most dragons rarely think about accounting. But you've worked hard to acquire that hoard of gold and jewels--shouldn't you be keeping track of what happens to it? Just sitting on it isn't good enough any more. That's why you need accounting. Here are some tips:

Tip One: A Copper Saved Is a Copper Earned

Your hoard isn't just valuable to you; it's valuable to thieves. Once word gets out that you're sitting on a big pile of treasure, it isn't long before they come skulking about, their greedy hands trying to snatch the things you've gained through honest plunder.

Dragons may have the reputation of knowing every single item in their hoard, down to the last copper, but the fact of the matter is that only a tiny fraction of dragons can remember more than six or seven thousand individual pieces before they all start to blur together. Admit it--you really aren't sure whether you have twenty-seven ruby-encrusted platinum goblets, or only twenty-six.

But thanks to proper accounting, you can have a complete inventory of everything in your hoard. That way, if you find something is missing, you can go on a rampage across the countryside or demand a virgin as a sacrifice unless your treasure is returned.

Tip Two: Plan for Taxes

The Dragon King will always demand his share, but you need to remember it's your hoard, not the king's. There are legitimate deductions you can take to reduce the amount you pay in taxes.

For example, did you know that knight insurance can be written off as a legitimate expense? Defending yourself against the pests in plate-mail is something that happens in the ordinary course of business. A good knight insurance policy will cover not only dents in your scales and arrows through your wings, but also full reimbursement for any treasure you have to give out to make the knight go away.

Many dragons forget that alternative forms of income, such as virgin sacrifices, are also taxable, and they get a nasty surprise when the tax bill arrives. Plan to set aside some treasure to cover the extra taxes.

. . .

Tip Three: Keep Good Records

In case of a tax audit, you need to have good records. But that's not the only reason.

Imagine the following scenario. You swoop down out of the sky onto some innocent village. Your teeth and talons are sharpened. Your breath is smoky fresh. But before you can rend flesh from bone and set the buildings ablaze, some village elder comes out with documentation showing they sacrificed a virgin to you earlier in the year. It's enough to make you slink away with your tail dragging in the mud.

You can avoid such embarrassment by recording all of your income, including sacrificial virgins. Note down the amount, the source, and the date.

Good recordkeeping also allows you to be more proactive. For example, you may notice that a particular village is late in offering a sacrifice. Then it's your choice whether to demand an immediate sacrifice or go wreak havoc on the village.

Tip Four: Hire a Good Accountant

Maybe you're just too busy. Or maybe you're bad at math. For whatever reason, you may decide to hire an accountant rather than do the work yourself. Generally, you have two options when it comes to hiring an accountant.

A good dragon accountant can be expensive, although he usually pays for himself through tax savings.

For the more cost-conscious dragon, a smarter choice is to find a human accountant who will gladly do all your accounting without charging you a single copper, simply in return for not being eaten. Over the long term, the savings can really add up.

———

"That's the end," I said after I finished reading the brochure. The echo of my voice faded away inside the cave.

"I'd never realized the advantages," said the dragon. Its black tongue flickered out to moisten its scaly lips. "After I eat you, I'll have to find myself an accountant."

I cleared my throat. "By sheer coincidence," I said, "it turns out that I'm an accountant. That's why I just happened to have that brochure with me."

"An accountant?" The gold and jewels of the dragon's hoard sparkled as he snorted flame. "The village elders claimed you were a virgin!"

"Strange as it may seem," I said, "the two are not mutually exclusive."

"Oh," said the dragon. "Well, then, I suppose you'll do. You'll work for not being eaten?"

"I would find that quite satisfactory," I said. "Plus, there's a substantial tax benefit to you, because an uneaten virgin sacrifice doesn't count as income. Now, let's review your financial situation. I'll need to see your tax returns for the past three years, your current knight insurance policy . . ."

"But I don't have a knight insurance policy," said the dragon.

"Really? You're in luck." With a broad smile, I reached into my pocket. "I just happen to have a brochure called <u>Insurance for Dragons</u>."

IF LOOKS COULD KILL, IT WOULD HAVE BEEN US INSTEAD OF HIM

BY GARRETT COOK

KILL shot gets the pearl kill shot gets the pearl kill shot gets the pearl kill shot gets the today it's going to be kill shot gets the pearl

Tyler did not have anything else in his head for more or less the duration of the shift. The other guys might have been every bit as single-minded and they might have had just as much need for the pearl but this mattered little to a man with a woman like Joanna at home and no real aptitude save for spotting far away objects and killing them. Given the chance to go home with the pearl, he could think of nothing else.

The sky was grey and threatened rain, big rain

perhaps, buckets, boatloads, puddles that promised canals. The sky of late had been good at keeping promises. The sky, though pregnant with dreams of drowning, was clear of any targets, not even so much as a seagull for some young swinging hardon to blow out of the sky just to kill his boredom. The sky was vacant and ominous and good for nobody but maybe this was an omen. Maybe this was their way of saying they were on their way.

One lucky shot and he could leave this work forever, like Guerrero. Kill shot gets the pearl and the pearl gets you free. He watched the nothing, the threatening grey and in those shifting clouds, he saw nothing more than the promise of freedom from war and work and want.

"Not today," said Masha, popping her gum, "you should go home. See your lady."

He looked her in her one good eye, all severity and judgment.

"Fuck you, I know what you're doing."

She flipped him off.

"Fuck you right the fuck back. Nothing to gain from being up here another two hours."

"It's mine. You won't psych me out of it."

The Russian shrugged square, strong shoulders.

"Suit yourself."

"We will not give up on them," said Heaven.

Without blame.

The young dragon held this deep. This was important, more important than anything. He took pride in resplendent golden scales and whiskers that extended long behind him. He took pride in the bright, shining pearl in his mouth but most of all, he took pride in the place that he had been given and the tasks set out before him. The dragons of the sky were limitless in compassion and limitless in the lengths they went to serve and proliferate compassion. The superior beast does not judge or place judgment above need.

The young dragon had heard others of its kind rumble their disdain for man's mistakes and had heard them say that the duties of Heaven were not for this world any longer. He had heard their doubts and nearly let them stoke his own but could not. These were not the actions of a superior beast and this did not acknowledge that to the superior man or beast, lesser men and beasts were without blame, always without blame.

Like all who would first embark on sacred tasks or duties that could end in bloodshed, the young dragon was of course afraid as it descended from Heaven and prepared to go forth and calm the waters but in its fiery jewel of a heart, it held more deeply that he was not to give up on mankind as the lesser dragons whispered that they should. The world below was teeming with the sounds of sobs and sighs and gunfire, the sounds of suffering.

It is one thing to think mankind is without blame without knowing mankind, it is another to listen to them and think such a thing. In the sounds of war and despair and loss, it understood the protestations of the dragons below and the desire to abandon them altogether to stay in the heavens.

———

The rain came down hard and promised no respite from rain.

The rain came down and said it wouldn't forget and couldn't forgive.

The rain spoke to the river and said "now is your chance." The water could take back the life that had so defiantly crawled from its arms and proceeded to take instead from the land. The river was angry and lonely and ravenous for souls. It listened to the rain, took it in and reached cold, grasping tendrils onto the land and up into foundations and into homes. They had dared to assume they'd made peace. That could not be. Joanna asked that God make sure he came home. The Chinese had sent their most ferocious demons. She asked that he spare her the waters rising and threatening conquest. She asked what she had done wrong so that she might atone. There was nothing she would not do to atone. She needed His protection from the rain the Chinese demons brought and she needed her man to come home safe and sound. There was nothing she wouldn't do to atone but there was nothing she could do as well. Nothing listened but the water.

"Cunt," it hissed, "you give me no credit. I give you a chance to beg and you talk to your God instead. No God makes floods. The flood is God unto itself, you callow bitch."

She prayed and cried as it seeped into the basement. She'd had her chance. The river listened no longer.

"You're not a good enough shot. You should be grateful just to have this job," said Skunk, yawning and stretching, "every asshole on the wall thinks he's bringing home a pearl. Won't be you."

The old man was psyching Tyler out like Masha. He

saw in the clouds a chance to get out of town and make everyone proud of him and to feel like someone for the first time since leaving the service. He had been a shitty line cook, then a poor cashier and now was back to being a pretty good sniper who could be known as a great sniper. He would be the one everyone on the wall envied and talked about come the following Monday.

"Fuck you, old man, you just want me to lose focus."

Skunk shook his head.

"No, I want you to understand that these is the end times. There's a great flood comin' and we ain't gonna stop it. The rain will come, dragons or none. And when it does, what we do here won't be worth shit. You come to the wall lookin' for fortune. None to be had."

The Chinese sent dragons. The dragons sent rain, which was coming down fierce now. The men on the wall stopped the dragons who would surely come with the rain. The men on the wall stopped the rain. The rain would stop and the pearl would fix his life. The thought that his fiancée was at home as the rains came down tried to intrude but was bounced at the door by dreams of riches and relevance. He watched the clouds as the rains began to soak him to the bone.

"Go home," said Masha.

"Go home," said Skunk.

"Fuck you both. The pearl's mine."

His comrades on the wall laughed as he shivered, clothes drenched and sticking to him. Fuck them all, this was about love.

———

Without blame.

They did not know what they did. They could not

know the dreams of an angry river or why the sky torrented tears. They could not speak and assuage the waters, that wasn't their duty. The heavens had sent the dragons in all their splendor to do this and though he heard foul things from their mouths and hearts, he was not deterred. He drew close to the men at the giant wall, close enough to hear the water but not close enough to be heard. Beyond the wall, he could reach the wall and soothe it with words and secrets known only to dragons. Cruel as men, the waters would be crueler.

In one man's heart, the resplendent one saw a hope that moved it deeply. This was mankind at their best, an imperfection, striving toward the superior. It flew nearer and felt warmth and hope in this most hopeful of hearts and took pride in knowing it could preserve lives like this one. If only men had spoken the language of dragons, then maybe they could have communicated and appreciated each other for who they were.

As it approached the wall, it went where many of its kind had gone before. At this place, the hope they brought came only from the pearls they kept clamped in their jaws. The dragon was seen as punishment from foes beyond the sea and had treasure and fame to offer, which filled the hopeless with promise of never working again. This, the dragon saw as longing for the order of the Earth to be restored.

"Don't worry," it wished it could say, "soon, everything will be fine and the storm will be calm at last."

But the time of men and dragons speaking had passed. Self-sufficient man built his world and his cities without need for the servants of the skies. Secrets and platitudes, poems and promises were shared in that language for centuries and there was love and goodwill between them. He wished he could understand where this connection had gone but no dragon would answer, no cloud and no peak would talk about those days anymore.

He spiraled and trembled and almost lost his place in the air when he drew closer and felt beyond the hope. Terror, desperation, need that could never be met. These were the creatures the dragons of Earth and Fire spoke of, the slayers of many of his kin.

———

Tyler was not the first to shoot. He'd been ill prepared. The dragons he'd seen were a thunderhead grey like the clouds he'd grown far too accustomed to. This was a majestic whiskered serpent shining with splendor and power and promise. The glint off those scales as it broke the monotony of the clouds and the stormy sky and a day of unbridled tedium all but blinded him. He could have lost the pearl had it not flown so gracefully out of the way of the first volley of shots. It swam the sky as fish swam water, more accustomed to flight than they were to shooting down dragons.

For a second he swore it was looking at him, pleading with him. It had to be a trick. China was cunning and China had sent the dragons to send the rain. He could not be fooled by this base deception, not even by the tear in its giant eye. It kept trying to fly on ahead anyhow, which was a surefire sign that it had been full of shit. He saw an opening and he took aim, giving birth to a shot that would hopefully mean an end to this flying devil and an end to China sending dragons and an end to the rain and an end to poverty.

Then through the shining eye the bullet went, the wise, compassionate, hurt and angry eye. From there, it continued on its journey. It burrowed through hard skull, sword-breaking skull. Bone and blood-stained burnished gold, divine perfection sullied by gore and greed and lies and need. It opened its jaws to roar in pain and dropped to the wall its precious pearl, the thing its killer longed for more than life itself. While it could still think it did its very best to make its final thought the one by which it lived.

"Without blame," it thought while it could still think.

"You're a goddamned fool," thought the churning waters below as it fell to an earth.

Tyler leaned down and now held in his hands a literal piece of Heaven, a chance at a new tomorrow. He ignored the beast splashing down into an overflowing river battering into the wall, he ignored the final texts still unanswered on his phone. He accepted the claps on his back and the cheering of his comrades on the wall and their knowledge that he could now move on to bigger and better. He looked again out on the horizon at the future not knowing it was washing away beneath him.

THE BLACK DRAGON
BY JUSTIN A. BURNETT

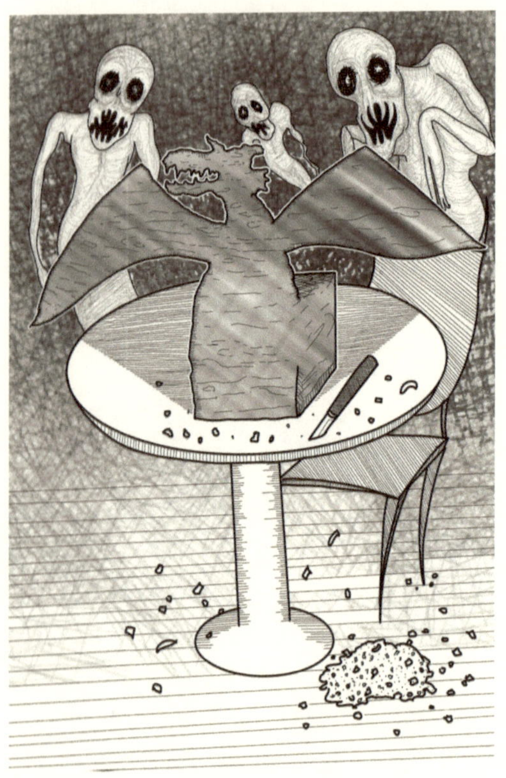

As HIS HANDS collide against a Mason jar full of pens, spilling them onto the kitchen floor with a clatter he was unprepared for, Kurt suddenly remembered gripping his son's shoulders one June afternoon and giving them a firm shake. It was the tremor in his hands, those uncooperative, rebellious extensions of his flesh, that must've inspired the unexpected resurgence of that dreary dusk when the day's work had just ended by the drowning of the sun against the flat, blue plane bristling with stalks of wheat. It was a mistake, he realized now, to touch the boy like that, although Kurt wondered if he could've done differently given the circumstances. What circumstances? The usual, certainly: exhaustion weighing against him like a bad conscious, a numb paralysis radiating from the bone and infecting his muscle tissue. In a word, Kurt blamed the limitations of his body for failing to tolerate the boy's playfulness after Kurt had ordered him back to the house. And what recourse does one have against the almighty corpus? The greatest argument against free will, Kurt believed, is its contingency on slowly dying matter.

Kurt ignores the pens rolling maliciously across the floor in search of the kitchen's many inaccessible crannies and returns to the block of wood. The knife in his hand blurs into an indefinite sliver of bending light as he tries to hold it steady. "Goddamn sickness," he mutters to the empty trailer. If there was one thing Kurt once revered as immune to the tyranny of the body, it was the dragons. They lined the trailer, held aloft by large nails and wooden pegs driven into sheets of plywood leaning against the fragile drywall. In the hard years after the woman's death and the equally irreversible and cruel departure of the children into adulthood, the dragons had occupied the excess of time in which Kurt found himself suddenly imprisoned. He began making them almost by accident. In a paroxysm of anxiety, he whittled away at a block of mesquite until he was surprised by an emerging form.

The blade first exhumed the vague outline of a serpentine body; scales appeared next, then wings. Strange that his square and thoroughly practical farmer's hands almost effortlessly sought an expression of such superfluous grace. Kurt recalled no childhood affinity to dragons, and he certainly didn't have time afterwards to indulge in tales of fantastic creatures. His childhood, like that of his girl and boy, had always been subject to the utilitarian needs of brutal, hard working adults. Fantasy was a luxury of the shiftless city folk; it had no place on the farm. Nevertheless, somehow, without seeking it, he had discovered the pleasure of gentle curves, a thrilling contrast to the hard and angular contours of the trade tools that had accompanied him through life. The only point of connection between the oceanic swells of scaly flesh materializing like magic beneath the worn blade of the Old Timer and the procession of indistinguishable days forming the hollow container of Kurt's past was the wheat; when the golden sea bent under the palpitations of the east wind, the glistening patterns were scales along a dragon's spine.

The sky grew cinereous through the parted curtains above the kitchen sink as Kurt tried once more to steady the block of black walnut between his knees. He had shaken the boy and karma had carried the echoes of his impatience across time, depositing a fossilized remnant of his fury in the neurons connecting the disobedient hands to his brain. "The tremors are your own damn fault," Kurt told himself, but the small comforts of justice blanched sheepishly against the mounting frustrations of incompletion.

He was determined to finish the black dragon. Decades had passed in preparation; wood shavings had gathered in increments measurable by the centimeter on pages of books left open to chapters on the mušḫuššu of the Mesopotamians, the Egyptian Apep, the Hebrew Leviathan, and Jörmungandr of Norse mythology. The slender, wingless dragons of the East adorning the cover of hardbacks forming two opposing walls around the sink had faded to pastel shades in the sun. "Decades," Kurt groaned to the empty room. Decades of fanatical attention to detail, intensive reading, of insulating the maddening womb of solitude with the consoling anticipation of a masterpiece. The knife tumbled from his hands and clattered against the table. "No tears," he commanded, forcing his anarchist biology to grope uselessly over the fallen blade, "are you not a man?"

The sudden crash against the outside wall of the trailer could be mistaken for the impact of a human palm, but Kurt knew better. He resisted the urge to stumble to the blinds and close them, forcing his eyes not to glance into the looming dusk creeping across the untended wheat. He strangled the electric swell of fear before it reached his throat, and returned to the block of black walnut.

Kurt knew the walnut would be nearly impossible to carve. It was as tough as stone, allotting the blade only small gouges and nicks in return for its efforts. But, also like stone, it was immortal. If there was one thing Kurt knew and tried to bequeath to his children, it was that nothing worthwhile comes without effort. Had he successfully taught them this? It seemed likely to Kurt that he had failed here as he had failed everywhere else; he had certainly failed the girl, who now passed between the hands of drunk men like a greasy wad of cash, men who unanimously proved too chickenshit to pay Kurt the courtesy of a proper visit. The boy seemed content enough with his wife and his big bank job and his spacious apartment in the heart of a city where everything remained comfortably within his purchasing power. Content enough, that is, without Kurt. But Kurt remembered the boy's restless gaze six years ago; his brilliant blue eyes had quickly assessed Kurt's trailer and the family farm in terms of real estate value; the boy silently regarded the dragons as variables in an equation dividing collector prices by the months Kurt's life work would likely accumulate dust in an expensive storage shed. Kurt swore the boy's shoulders had visibly sagged with disappointment at the result. The old man doubted whether a life wasted under the spell of acquisition could truly be happy.

Another impact echoed through the trailer, louder this time. As the windows rattled faintly in the aftershock, Kurt redoubled his struggles with the dark slab of stony wood. Steadying the knife with both hands, he made a tentative assault on the unyielding surface. Small gouges began to appear; the exhumation had begun. Suddenly, the sinuous twists of the black dragon's body buried in the limpid heart of walnut glowed so clearly that Kurt momentarily imagined he already held the finished product between his knotted hands. He lifted it to the feeble kitchen light, and the dragon's scales caught the glow like a diamond. Could it truly be over? he asked himself. Have I finally vindicated the debt of failures heedlessly accumulated over a lifetime? Oh wise black dragon, revered harvester of the final autumn, have you come to relieve me of my memory? the hours spent preoccupied by the greedy soil as the girl traced the fence line, laughing at the neighboring brood of boys? my own boy's tears, backlit by the purple bruise of impending night as my thumbs wedge fiercely into the soft flesh above his collarbone? and the woman, oh god, her fever, the insurmountable doctor's expenses, gray eyes dimming as the sun climbs to the zenith, the white outline of salt shaped like an egg left behind on the dark couch during the empty months that followed?

The illusion faded as abruptly as it came. The chipped walnut block in Kurt's trembling hands no longer reflected the jaundiced kitchen light; the black dragon was buried, once again, beneath the forbidding layer of dead cells.

As Kurt lowered the block to the table, he glimpsed an ashen face in the kitchen window just as it ducked out of sight. A moment later, something crashed viciously against the front door. Down the hall and beneath the floor, a thunder of furious pounding answered, sending tremors through the flimsy trailer house walls.

Kurt sits alone in the roaring din of fists against the outside of the trailer. Despite his fear, a song that he may have heard in a long lost childhood rings maniacally in his head: *they're coming to take me away, ha ha, they're coming to take me away, ho ho*…. Slowly, he rises from his chair. His legs tremble now, not from the sickness, but in terror. Nevertheless, he forces himself to the window. Against the remnants of the last daylight hours of his life, Kurt sees the gray figures crawling through the wheat, cutting shadowed crevices from the horizon that converge on the lonely trailer. The luminous red of their eyes fills the window and reflects vaguely from their long, unnaturally sharpened teeth. "I'm too late," Kurt whispers breathlessly as he staggers back to his chair.

He always thought the could beat them. They first appeared when his hands began to shake, and he knew intuitively they foreshadowed his end. Only the black dragon, the prince of silent deaths, could save him. Kurt forces his hands to the piece of black walnut. The pressure of tears brings a familiar pain to his eyes, and he almost succumbs. What, after all, has been the source of his failures if not his slavish adherence to manhood? What good has it done to sacrifice his life to work, his attention to duty? Hadn't his life been ruined by his stubborn inability to tell the woman how much he loved her before she was gone? Cry, then, if you must! Weep, since it is your final chance! But old habits don't die hard; they refuse to die at all, and Kurt steels himself against the increasing convulsions of the trailer, the groan of the wood, and plunges the knife into the block.

The walnut deflects the blade and sends it diving into the meat of his leg. A moment of shock clears his mind; the trailer falls silent, the creatures outside vanish, and Kurt slumps heavily against the worn edge of the kitchen table before collapsing onto the linoleum. The space surrounding his heart frantically contracts, strangling his lungs as a new web of pain spreads into his extremities like a hand slipping into a glove. Soon there is light, and Kurt relaxes his grip on the boy, pulling his fingers away from the soft, tender flesh. "I'm sorry," he says, staring fiercely into the blue eyes while his own glisten with tears. "I'm sorry for everything," he says, and Kurt reaches for a pen on the floor near his right hand. On the bottom of the table, he writes the words as he says them, despite the wild spasms of his muscles. The boy points to the brightening white of the sun, and Kurt turns to watch a black dragon unfold along the crest of brilliant light.

CREATION

BY JESSICA AMANDA SALMONSON

"They roar like Tehomoth."

— ISAIAH 17:13

The Mother Dragon Tiamat
Drew Chaos from Her depth
Then issued every dream and
        thought
From her vaginal cleft.

She rose up as Leviathan
Earth pendant from Her fin
And knit the universe as One
From pieces wrought within.

A DRAGON IN ONYX

BY SETH HUNSAKER

THE CHEERS and shouts of the crowd as they lined the sidewalks of the French Quarter blended into the sounds of music and the parade that wandered its way along the road. The roaring cacophony was dulled by the flowing beer that passed from tap to cup to belly and by the drugs secreted in shadowed alleys or passed under the tables in the back of dives. The rattle of beads turned heads skyward as they sought topless women along the balconies while shouts, and the whoops of Krewe members rang out as they passed along on floats tossing strands to bystanders. Men and women stood shoulder to shoulder with one another, laughing and hollering, cheering and drinking together.

Along a small side alley, beneath a thin-striped canopy, a man stood hidden in a doorframe, the close walls and canopy shielding him from the flickering lights of neon signs. His cobalt-colored eyes scanned the crowd of party-goers as they passed across the alley heading from one bar to the next. His gaze settled on a lone female, a bag clutched to her chest in a protective manner. Slipping from his cover, the man moved into the street and blended with a crowd of costumed tourists walking towards a nearby hotel for one of the many Mardi Gras Masquerade Balls that were held nightly. He merged into the crowd and followed behind the woman a few paces back, not wishing to draw attention to himself just yet. Darting to the left quickly, the woman began to run as fast as she could. With a curse the man burst through the tourists and sprinted after her. His mind filled with questions of how she had fingered him and when.

Pushing past revelers, the man hadn't noticed until too late the large two-by-four swinging from a side alley. Clipping his jaw, the wooden plank slipped from the woman's hands and clattered to the pavement as she shrieked in pain. Slumping against a wall, the man groaned as his vision swirled for a moment. Shaking himself from his delirium, he turned to see the girl cradling one of her hands in the other as she backed down the alley. The bag hung from one of her arms by a thin leather strap, its mate dragging the ground in a broken tatter. Her eyes darting side-to-side, the woman noticed the wrought iron bars that blocked a part of the alley off. She kicked at them in desperation.

"Damn it! I was told everything was fixed! Mickey

said he had the cops on his payroll! What are ya, some kind of shining knight? My hands broken cause of you," the girl rambled as she continued to kick the bars, probing for a loose one she could knock free to make an escape. Her hazel eyes were wide with fear and adrenaline. The chase and subsequent hand injury had flooded her brain with endorphins, putting her nerves on high alert. Looking at her cradled left hand, the man noticed the ring finger was bent at an unnatural angle, a reddish-purple shade spreading along the joint as it began to swell.

With a sigh, the man drew a leather wallet from his back pocket and held it up. The heavy, steel, star-shaped badge was polished to a perfect shine and reflected the light of an overhead street lamp from golden finish. The words 'ORLEANS PARISH DEPUTY' were etched in black enamel along the circumference of the star. "I'm Deputy Mattias Raske. Drop the bag and put your hands up." His accent sounded odd to the girl, not like those of the common folk of Louisiana. His was from another country. Eastern European, she guessed. "Oh, please, Mister Lawman. Don't get rough with little ol' me,-" she said sarcastically.

With a deep sigh, Mattias produced a set of steel cuffs and stepped towards the girl. Cuffing her took only a moment, despite her attempts to pull away. Once she had been secured, Mattias pulled a cell phone from his pocket and called for backup. The polished, white squad car that showed up 10 minutes later was adequate to transport them to Headquarters. Mattias wanted to get the troublesome woman booked but began to feel a twinge in his stomach. The feeling that his night was not going to go as planned nagged at him.

Mattias radioed into the station and asked to be

patched through to the Sheriff. "Yeah Raske, what is it?" Sheriff Bonits was halfway across New Orleans, situated in a warehouse office waiting for the informant to arrive so that the sting could begin in earnest. Mattias knew that he was about to be rebuked for the words that he felt needed to be said, but he had to ensure he did everything he could to stop the feeling of unease building inside him.

"Hey boss. We got the girl and what she was carrying. We're taking her in now, but I have a bad feeling about this whole thing. Like we just stepped into something that is going to land us in a world of hurt. I think we shouldn't go through with the rest. We should just take the package and get a warrant for the morning." Mattias let the silence fill the car for a second before letting the "send" button go on the radio. With a deep sigh, the sheriff began to speak low.

"Raske, you're a good boy and one hell of a deputy. But we gotta nip this in the bud or else Mickey Parks and his crew are going to be causing some shit for us that we don't want."Raske had made it back to the Sheriff's office within the half hour. It wasn't until after he had gotten the girl booked and into a cell when the call came through from Sheriff Bonits. The radio crackled with interference, but the Sheriff's words still came through. "Mickey Parks and all his crew are dead, butchered in their own hideout. Drugs and such is all still here as is the money we had watched that mule of his grab from the dead drop."

Raske looked at the radio as he heard the Sheriff speak. Mickey Parks was no John Gotti, but he was also not some hood banger with a cheap 9 Millimeter and a 40-ounce bottle of malt liquor. To hear that he and all his men had been cut down like wheat before the thresher was unsettling to Mattias. "Holy shit! Do we have any clues who did this?" Mattias asked. "Not yet. Still a lot to comb through here," Sheriff Bonits answered in a cold manner. Mattias sighed and the spoke earnestly. "I got the girl, Caroline Erickson, into a cell and stored the package she had in the lockup. Do you want me to go talk to her or wait until you get here?"

Mattias listened to the silence of the radio. "No, go talk to her. Figure out who'd do this. I'll be here for more than an hour or so cleaning this mess up."

Leaving the radio, Mattias headed toward the Round House, the lock-up for the Sheriff's Department. Unlocking the door, Mattias walked slowly into the white cement-walled room and noticed that something was off. At the end of the well-lit hall, a thin hand stretched through the bars of a cell, clutching at the air before spasming once and falling slack. Running furiously down the hall, Mattias struggled to free his keys. Sliding to a stop, Mattias slipped a key into the cell's lock. With a loud clanking bang, the door slid open on an old track gear and came to a rest in the open position.

Leaning down, Mattias grabbed Caroline's slack form and tugged her back into the cell, lifting her onto the metal bench that served as a makeshift cot. Bunching a pillow up under her head, Mattias got her into a position from which he could perform CPR if needed. Checking her pulse with one hand, Mattias opened one of her eyes with the other and checked her pupils. She was dead, a thin line of foam trailing from her lips and down her neck. Mattias stepped back and yelled for another deputy. After a moment, Deputy Lorneson came through the far door to the cell where Mattias stood beside the dead body of Caroline.

"Get a damn ambulance here and call the Sheriff

now. Tell him the girl is dead. Poison, by the looks of it. I need to go to lockup and make sure whatever she was carrying is still here." Mattias left the cell and stormed through the door. He wanted to know how someone got through the door to the Round House and poisoned the girl without anyone noticing. Stepping through another door into a small, grey-washed hallway light with buzzing fluorescent lights, Mattias pulled his keys out and selected a copper one. Slipping the tarnished key into the lock, he twisted the key and door knob, simultaneously opening the lockup.

Stepping in, Mattias flicked a small switch next to the door and illuminated the room around him. A large room, 20 feet long and 15 wide, stood before him. Shelves upon shelves lined the walls and stood in the middle of the room, forming an orderly grid of inventory. Guns, drugs, stolen goods, money, forged documents, and the lot all sat housed in specific boxes labeled carefully along the shelves. Stepping to the eighth shelf in the line, Mattias navigated his way to the small brown bag, grabbing it from its resting place, and made his way out.

His nerves were on edge now, and he had many questions that he wanted answers for. Glancing at the brown bag in his hand, he wondered if any of those answers were in there. Coming to the door that led to the front, Mattias noticed it was open a crack. He had shut the door behind him as he went to the lockup, and the Round House was at the rear of the building, so Lorneson hadn't been through. Drawing his pistol, Mattias slowly pushed open the door and stepped in, the barrel of his Glock leading the way. Creeping down the hall that entered the front of the building, Mattias heard Lorneson talking to someone. Leaning around the corner, Mattias could see the shape of a person wearing all black standing between him and Lorneson, whose hands were in the air. In the reflection of a nearby window, Raske saw the shape of a SIG aimed at Lorneson's chest.

"I told you I don't know what you're talking about! The girl didn't have no bag on her when she was brought in! She's a known drug mule 'round here and probably tossed whatever she was carryin' in a drainage ditch or into a dumpster," Lorneson lied to the man despite the gun pointed at his heart. The man in black shifted his weight, his right hand balling into a fist and uncurling slowly. Raske could tell the man's patience was wearing thin.

"I am not stupid. I interrogated the bitch before she died. She told me a cop took the bag from her and brought it here. Now, that bag is very important to some very scary people who will bring this world to its knees to get their hands on it, so tell me where the bag is, Deputy, or else I will have no choice but to shoot you and then go look for the other cop that I saw bring her in. You have to the count of three. One… Two… Three—"

Realizing the man meant business, Mattias swung his whole body around the corner and hurled the bag as hard as he could toward the intruder yelling, "Catch, asshole!" The man in black spun around with a shocked expression on his face. Reaching both arms up to catch the bag hurtling towards his face, he did not see the gun in Raske's hand point directly at him until it was too late. With a squeeze of the trigger, Mattias fired a solitary round from his Glock.

Wide eyed, the intruder's head bucked with the force of the impact as the slug burrowed its way directly through his forehead and into his brainpan. Falling backwards, the black-clad body crumbled into a heap of flesh as the SIG thumped to the floor in the slack hand of the dead man. Lorneson stepped over the body and grabbed the bag just as it was about to hit the floor, holding onto it tightly by the leather strap. "Good lord, Raske. You must have a pair of brass and one hell of a confident ego to take a risk like that. This sumbitch coulda shot you, or worse, you could've missed him and shot me. Did ya think of that at all?"

Lorneson put the bag on a nearby desk and then leaned down to secure the intruder's gun. Mattias moved over and began to inspect the body. The man had no wallet on him or any form of identification. In the pockets of his clothes Mattias found a small syringe, 2 magazines of ammunition for his gun, and a small, pre-paid flip phone with no numbers saved in the contacts or call history. "Yes, Lorneson, I did think of those things, but he would have shot you had I not decided to do something. And while I might not like you somedays, I'd be sad if you were shot by some dirt bag."

Mattias moved to the desk, grabbing the bag nearby. As he took a seat, the unmistakable sound of Sheriff Bonits' truck could be heard pulling up front, followed by another vehicle. Within a minute, the Sheriff and two EMTs came through the door, pausing to look at the man lying dead on the floor. "What in the name of Mary and Joseph happened here?" Sheriff Bonits grumbled. Mattias explained the situation while Lorneson took the two EMTs into the Round House for the girl. Once Bonits had all the information, they both looked at the bag on the desk. "Open it up Raske. Time to see what the hell is so damned important that some nutcase would break into a Sheriff's Department and kill someone for."

Mattias unzipped the bag slowly, feeling it for any

indication of what could be inside. Then, he opened it wide and slipped its contents out. He had expected drugs or some other illegal item, but inside the bag was a small onyx statue. Picking it up, the Sheriff turned it over a couple times and then handed it to Mattias. The statue was made from some kind of black glass, with veins of green and blue material tracing the length of it. It was shaped into a dragon, with a long body like those portrayed in Asian mythology, but with a head, legs, and wings of a more European style. Speckled throughout the length of the statue were small mineral deposits that reflected light from all angles, making it seem that within the onyx body of the statue, swirls of stars twinkled deep within.

Setting it down, Mattias sighed with frustration and looked at the Sheriff. "So, all this over some damn bit of rock? There must be something more. Is it stolen? A rare piece from a museum?" Mattias now had more questions and still lacked answers. His mind raced with reasons why this chunk of carved rock could be so important, but he could not settle upon a plausible possibility.

Staring at the statue, Mattias was reminded of a popular book by a New England author named Lovecraft he saw in the windows of more eclectic bookstores. He'd skimmed it once, and remembered it was well loved due to a chapter set in New Orleans and the surrounding swamp. The premise of the chapter regarded a small statue made of some green stone worshipped by backwoods degenerates who killed for the thing. He wondered how many had died for this particular statue. He imagined the voices of people screaming as their lives were snuffed out in some horrible manner. Then he heard a voice within him. "Free... me...." Shaking himself from his thoughts, Mattias stared at the statue again and then looked at the clock. It was near one in the morning and he had not seen much sleep the night before. *Just my imagination,* he thought as he stretched a kink from his neck. "I think I am going to go home and go to bed. Tomorrow feels like it's going to be a very long day." Mattias nodded to the Sheriff and then left the station.

The next morning greeted Mattias with a bright spring day and a call from the sheriff, who informed him that a man in a dark suit with blonde hair had showed up to the Sheriff's department. He had introduced himself as Special Agent Johannes Brandt with the FBI. After arriving to the office, Sheriff Bonits and Mattias spoke to the man and explained the events of the night before. Agent Brandt simply listened and took notes. His stoic demeanor made Mattias think of the stereotypical G-man who pushed papers and kept a tight lip about anything he saw or heard. Mattias respected the man's position as a government lawman, but his interest in an attempted armed assault and theft of a Sheriff's Department made Mattias suspicious.

Once a rundown of the night's events had been given, Brandt asked to see the statue. Mattias brought it out of his desk drawer and placed it before the man. Turning the carved statue in his hand, Agent Brandt examined it from top to bottom and then placed it back on the desk.

"I see. Sheriff, from here on out I will be taking over the investigation into this incident. I will need all the evidence in relation to this case, as well as access to the body of the intruder immediately. I will also require Deputy Raske to assist me. I will have the papers from my department forwarded to you immediately providing me with full jurisdiction here." Brandt smiled lightly, then turned and left.

Later that day, Mattias was called to the city morgue on the north end of town where he was met by Agent Brandt. After exchanging formalities, the two entered the morgue and made their way to the front desk.

Sitting inside was a young woman, no more than 28 years old. Her long auburn hair was tied back in a ponytail, her brown eyes staring at the two men from behind a small set of wire frame glasses. As they had entered, the woman took a quick glance in a small compact mirror she kept hidden beneath the lip of the counter. As Mattias and Brandt passed the entrance and stopped before the girl, Mattias noted how she seemed to be looking the two men over. It was apparent to anyone that they were not partners normally, and that this was a simple 'keep your friends close' type of moment.

Standing before the pair, the woman gave a slight bow of her head and then smiled. After she had verified them, the young woman buzzed them through the door and led them to the small room where the coroner had the body of an Alexander Toomes, the gunman from the night before, brought for inspection. As they walked, she introduced herself. "My name is Cybil Forestier. You were called here because we have a problem. Shortly after the body arrived last night, it was stolen by some fiend along with the possessions that were brought in as well." Her voice contained a note of revulsion at the thought that someone would break into the morgue to steal remains. After entering the small ceramic and steel-lined coroner's room, Brandt and Raske searched all around but found no sign of who had done this or why. It was as if the body seemed to have gotten up and left of its own accord. With no choice left at hand, Brandt knew he needed to drop the subterfuge.

"Despite your silence on this odd matter, Deputy Raske, I feel I need to be candid with you now. The things we have stepped into are much deeper than the nearby bayou, and even more deadly. I introduced myself as Special Agent Johannes Brandt of the FBI. This is not quite the truth. I am Special Agent Johannes Brandt, but I am not with the FBI." Mattias looked the man up and down with a look of confusion. "Then who are you with? NSA? CIA? Homeland?" The question hung on the air for a moment as Brandt formulated his next words. "I am with the Department of Defense's special division known as B.O.W.R.I, or Bowery as we call it."

Leaning across the table, Raske lifted an eyebrow and then looked Agent Brandt up and down. "What the hell is Bowery and why have we never heard of it?" Raske spoke coolly. He looked at Brandt and simply waited. "The Bureau for Occult Warfare, Research, and Investigations. The Bureau was formed during the first days of America's founding, during the Revolution, to fight against the horrors brought forth by the Crown. Since that time, we have secretly existed in the shadows, doing what is needed by the U.S. Government. As to the events of late, I am just as much in the dark as you. But someone wants the statue, and whoever they are, they sent a Cleaner to retrieve the statue."

Just as Brandt had finished speaking, the sounds of automatic weapon fire rang out in three short bursts. Slipping from the room, Brandt and Raske made their way across the wall and into sightline of the front entrance. Standing at the entrance, two men clad in black stood with guns in their arms. Brandt knew who they were immediately: a kill squad sent after Raske and the statue. Looking to Raske, Brandt whispered softly, "They are here for you, and by extension, me, and probably the statue."

As if on cue, one of the men yelled out towards the back of the bank. "I know you're both there, Deputy, Special Agent. The Sheriff was quite candid with your location."

Raske tensed up at the man's words, knowing the Sheriff had come to harm. Brandt sensed his anger and put a hand on him. In a clear tone, Brandt asked, "Why do you want the statue? Is it some museum piece worth a high price?" He knew better but felt best to distract the armed men from the fact that they had the advantage now.

"I am Helbrecht of the Knights of the Golden Era, and we seek the idol of our God. The statue will unlock the key needed to release it from eternal slumber. Now give us the idol!" Helbrecht yelled ferociously. Gunfire spat from the doorway, pinging from the steel frame and back wall in showers of sparks. Shaking his head, Brandt sighed. "I feared this was the case. More occultist nutjobs seeking some mythical key to unlimited power. Why can't it just be a simple case of Thaumaturgy gone wrong and a couple golems shambling around?" From Brandt's expression, Mattias felt these things were a norm for the Special Agent.

Mattias lifted an eyebrow at this companion but remained silent. In his head, he was calculating the scenario before him. The closest rooms to them were all inner rooms with no windows or secondary door. The well-armed gunmen were standing by the one and only entrance that did not require a key or passcode. Thankfully, they did not know that the statue sat no more than 300 feet away in Agent Brandt's car.

Thinking hard, an idea came to Raske that would work well if done right. Motioning to Brandt, the two crept along the wall and knelt, guns still at the ready. "I've got an idea, get ready!" Mattias pushed off the wall and jogged down the hall into the coroner's room. After a minute, he returned with a large bottle of embalming fluid affixed with a thin sheet of gauze tied around its thick neck. In his other hand, Mattias clutched a small box of matches. Brandt noted the small reddish-orange label with the swirl of black declaring the contents were flammable. Mattias could see the realization fall across Brandt's face as he realized what the plan was. Brandt looked as if he felt uneasy with the plan, but did not object.

Nodding his head to the entrance, Mattias handed the bottle to Brandt and then struck a match, holding it at a downward angle so the head would catch and burn enough lighting the gauze. Whipping his hand around, Raske put the match out and then snagged the flaming bottle from Brandt with a quick motion.

Mouthing the words '1, 2, 3.' Raske spun and lobbed the makeshift Molotov over the receptionist desk and into the main lobby. With a crash of broken glass, the bottle burst against the hard-tiled floor and splashed some of its contents about. With a 'whoosh', the flames caught the embalming solution alight and sent tendrils of greasy acrid smoke through the room. The two men, Knight Helbrecht and his unnamed companion, saw the fire and jumped back in a panic. Too late did they realize that the flames were merely a decoy.

Spinning from their hiding place with guns drawn

and aimed straight, Raske and Brandt took the marksman stance, the sights of their weapons trained on the center of mass of their targets. "Drop the weapon, Helbrecht! We will shoot if you so much as move wrong." Brandt's normally soft, friendly tone had vanished, and razor-sharp steel hardened his voice. Raske kept the unknown assailant in his sight and watched for any sign of resistance or intent to bring weapons to bare from the men. Helbrecht simply smiled as he and his partner did the unthinkable. As one, both men brought their rifles up and squeezed off a series of rounds. The shots went wild as both Raske and Brandt fired with deadly precision, bringing the stand off to a close.

Once the two intruders had fallen, Brandt rushed to them and began checking them for anything that could help uncover the whole story. Mattias worked to get the fire under control. With a due alacrity, Within a few short minutes, Mattias had the flames out. As he stood to his full height and breathed a sigh of relief, Brandt called to him.

Going to Brandt's side, what Mattias saw could not be possible. Lying beside the man known as Helbrecht was the body of Alexander Toomes. The 9-millimeter caliber hole in his forehead was still visible from the night before. "How the hell is this possible, Brandt?" Looking to the Special Agent, Raske felt his mind begin to slip into the harsh madness that the events of today had brought looming over his head like the Sword of Damocles. Brandt's reply held no reassurance. "The group these men work for are definitely not some common rabble or a zealous group of cultists who are so remote that a general education and the ability to find non-related breeding partners are impossible to find. They are rooted deep into insidious arts, so much so that they returned a pastiche semblance of life to the once-dead Alexander Toomes and returned him to his mission."

Mattias looked the two corpses over and tried not to think of the things weighing on him at this moment. Two days prior, the world made sense to him and he lived blissfully unaware of any of this anarchy. Yet now he stood knee-deep in pointed hats, malign ancient beings who looked like mythological dragons, and men and women who could return their comrades to life in order to hunt dissenters. "There is much work to be done still Deputy. Come along."

Gathering the bodies, the two men worked fastidiously to enclose them within body bags found in a nearby room. Hauling them out, the two men placed them in the back of Mattias' squad car before returning to the morgue and gathering the rest of the two intruders' equipment. "The nearest deep swamp, where could we find that?" Agent Brandt spoke with a tone that denoted the next moments would be full of rocks, rope, and the heaving of the two black coroner's bags in the back.

Mattias thought for a moment then pointed north. "Well, there is a fairly deep bit of swamp a couple hours drive from here. Plenty of places to hide things. Why?" Looking Brandt square in the eyes, he waited patiently for the man to detail the plan. "There is no real way to remove the threat of that statue. I cannot take it, nor can you keep it. People would continue coming for it. It calls to them like a bell ringing. The only way to prevent them from getting it is to throw it away somewhere deep and dark, where it's siren call cannot reach out to them."

Two hours later, the sun had been reaching its zenith. The canopy of thick trees created patches of cool shade where their leaves and branches blocked the sun, cascading shadows through the murky swamp. Mattias stood beside Agent Brandt, their pants soaked to the knee from trudging through the deep waters as they carried the foul remains of the two men. A small bag with a broken strap hung from Mattias' left shoulder, it's contents tightly wrapped in thick cloth and covered in a strange solution Brandt had produced after a short stop at a small gas station.

With a final gaze around the swamp, Mattias pointed to a nearby outcropping of mud and weeds. "On the other side of that bit of land will be a large inlet pool that connects to a branch of the river north of here. It is rather deep and the dark soil at the bottom will help hide the bags." Mattias shifted his weight, then began hauling the one of the two coroner's bags to the plot of land he had pointed out. Brandt followed behind, dragging the second bag behind him. Reaching the mound of earth, the two men caught their breath and looked around.

"Well, let's finish this shall we?" Mattias said as he began lifting the coroner's bag into the nearby waters. Brandt grabbed the other end of the bag and hefted it up. With a quick swing, the two men hurled the laden bag and watched it begin to sink. The large rocks placed inside each bag would help keep the two bodies from rising to the surface. With one bag submerged, the two men turned and to the second bag and heaved it into the water a few feet from the other bag.

With the two bodies sunk, Brandt took the leather bag from Mattias and looked at it one last time. Using the broken strap, he tied a large stone to the bag and then hurled it far out into the pool. With a solid splash, the bag sunk immediately to the black depths of the pool, coming to rest within the sludge and muck. Turning away, the two men hiked back out of the swamp and found themselves back at their vehicles. Looking back at the swamp, Mattias sighed and shook his head. Brandt smiled and offered a hand to the deputy. "It was nice to meet you Raske. Please be safe and forget these last 2 days' experiences. They will cause nothing but madness and grief should you dwell upon them." Shaking the agent's hand, Mattias nodded. Without further words, the two men climbed within their separate vehicle and parted ways. Looking in his rearview mirror, Mattias watched as Brandt began to shrink into the distance while the sun began its descent towards the horizon.

ASHES FROM THE BEAST

BY MELANIE BOWLING

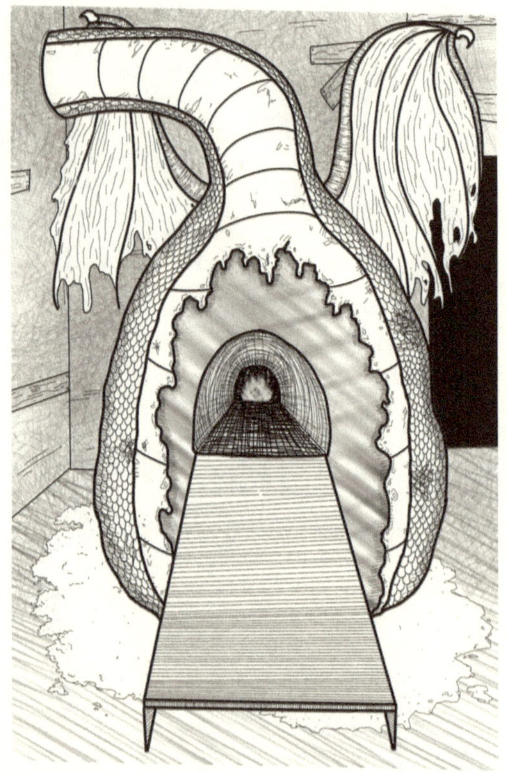

THE FOLLOWING journal entries are reproduced in completion. The journal was found buried in the White Mountains of New Hampshire in the summer of 2015 by a pair of hikers exploring the charred remnants of a village hidden in the woods.

August 27, 1998

I'm writing this diary because I don't know what is happening right now or if it'll even be noteworthy. If this is ever found, I want you to know that all of what is written here is true. If you do find this diary, it means

I'm dead and would not benefit from its contents being made public.

I guess I should probably introduce myself. My name is Matthew. I fancy myself a genius, but I'm really just average. Average. That's probably why my wife left me. I provided for her and cared for her, but she needed some excitement. Mentally and sexually, I guess. But less of me and more of why I'm writing this for you.

I can't help but wonder if my brain is fucking up again and I'm hallucinating this barn I'm hiding in and the citizens of this village. Whether it's real or not, I can't even begin to describe what I've discovered while wandering through this strange place. When I got here a couple weeks ago, I was a transient. Guess I still am, considering I have no permanent address to speak of. I left my home that I had worked hard to pay for when my wife left with the first guy she crushed on following our marriage. I had no reason to stay: a mind-numbing job and a mortgage I didn't even want in the first place. So, I left. Simply crammed a hiking bag full of anything that could fit, grabbed some granola bars and a camelpak and took off. Left my car and the house's doors unlocked. It's a new life!

It's not like the movies. Traipsing across the untamed United States isn't as freeing as you might believe. Criminals, shadows, and loneliness are a constant. Actually, if you find this diary, you're probably on the same path as me, so why the hell am I explaining this to you? There's so much to talk about. I'll start at the beginning tomorrow—after all, I need to save my flashlight battery.

August 28, 1998

One of the few things I miss about being at home is

a good cup of coffee. Blacker the better. None of that sweetener shit. I used to have it with a little milk, but that started messing up my stomach, so I switched to black and never looked back. I haven't had a good cup of coffee in about four months. At least my lack-of-caffeine tremors and headaches have finally subsided. Hiding out in this town has made me forget all about it anyway. I'm barely sustaining myself on something that appears to be bread, and stolen vegetables. My shits are like rocks, and that's only when I'm lucky enough to pass one. One thing I don't want is to die here.

The lack of food and clean water for the past two weeks probably hasn't been the best thing for my health. First of all, there's ash that pours out of a chimney in the center of town. Chunks of it, like large pieces of confetti. No one seems to notice, even though I'm constantly trying to get it out of my hair, my mouth, and off my clothes. It makes no sense to me. How do these people breathe and not realize they're inhaling more ash than oxygen? I'm honestly surprised that anyone can live here. The place doesn't seem habitable. I also don't think they realize what decade—or even century—they live in. They don't have electricity and I can't tell what clothing they wear, really, because it's all tinged gray from the ash raining down. Even their skin is pale and grayish.

I've noticed them taking bodies into the large, shed-like building the chimney is attached to. Maybe they're dying from the ash? I haven't really explored that area— I should tomorrow.

August 30, 1998

It's 3am and I'm waking up in my bed of hay. In my sleep, it hit me that the ash might be the dead bodies being burned in the shed. There are never funerals and I don't see a cemetery anywhere. Holy shit, I can't believe it just hit me! Must be the lack of nutrients. I will investigate when I'm more with it.

It's about 11pm right now. I stole some cabbage and pond water earlier and went over to the shed. I call it a shed, but it's really the size of a 2-bedroom house. Kinda dilapidated and thrown together with spare pieces of wood. No one could live here comfortably. That's because they fucking don't. No human lives here. I don't know if I believe anything I saw. 50/50 that I was hallucinating. Who knows what's in that pond water?

I walked through the front door and saw a steel oven that could easily cook 30 pizzas or 3 bodies, depending on what your goals are. It was like nothing I had ever seen. Surrounding this stove was the torso stump of a dragon. Scales, feathers, the whole bit. Thinking now, it's more like 70/30 I was hallucinating, but even then, it seemed so real. Holy fuck! If anyone reads this thing, just know that I saw a giant stove built into the lungs of a dragon. Not sure if it's even alive, but I'm investigating more tomorrow. I need to try to sleep and digest all this. It's the only thing I'll be digesting tonight, sadly.

August 31, 1998

I'm guessing it's about 9pm, since it got dark maybe an hour ago. I saw 4 bodies go into the shed and, I assume, into the chest of the dragon. I'm pretty positive now that I've been breathing the ashes of dead people. The man or woman (not sure which as they are cloaked and don't speak) wheels a body into the shed, then hoists them onto a manual conveyor belt. There's a very large handle they turn and the body moves to the stove. A bright fire blazes to life and a roar can be heard from the throat of the possibly dead dragon—I assume it's dead, but I'm by no means certain.

Thinking about it now, I'm wondering if the fire originates from the lungs of this dragon. Is the dragon's bottom half buried underground? I can't help but picture Satan half frozen in the ocean of ice in Dante's *Inferno* when I look at this thing. How is it staying alive if its lungs are pure fire? According to all the fairy tales, dragons breathe fire, so putting the bodies in the lungs makes sense. I'm not thinking clearly, again, obviously.

It's hitting me that I've been fucking breathing the ashes of dead people.

The chimney is built up from the lungs, through the throat, out the dragon's mouth, then out the shed's roof. The dragon is like that impaled girl in the movie *Cannibal Holocaust*, if you can picture that. The fire in the lungs burns the body, the chunks of ashes spill from chimney and, from there, make their way into the lungs of this place's citizens.

Out one set of lungs and into another.

September 2, 1998

I need to get the fuck out of here. I can't be in a place anymore with something like this happening. Keeping anything alive with dead bodies has to be immoral, right? Maybe they're just using what resources they have to their benefit. But if the people weren't forced to breathe ash they wouldn't die, and therefore wouldn't have to be put into the lungs of this beast, continuing the cycle. Why are they staying? Do they realize what they're breathing? Is it a new kind of evolution? I've noticed their pale skin, but I figured it was just because they were coated with the ashes pouring from the chimney. Maybe they ARE ash. Some sort of perverted animatronic of their former selves, like a super fucked-up Disney World exhibition. I wish that's all this was.

September 3, 1998

I think they know I'm here. I noticed that my things were out of place when I came back from taking a couple ash-potatoes from someone's crop. Is that a good or bad thing? Will the ash people take me in and take care of me or murder me? Considering it seems that everyone eventually dies, and that they don't even have funerals to honor their dead, they probably don't value human life much. IF they're human. I haven't actually interacted with any of them and I don't want to start now. They feed bodies to a dragon, for Christ's sake! I didn't even know they existed! Why would they let me leave if they're keeping this knowledge hidden? I can't be safe for long.

September 4, 1998

They know I'm here and they know I know about the dragon. I found a large tooth, almost the size of my hand, on my hay pile after I went to take my weekly bowel movement on the edge of town. I only go out at night and I never see anyone once the sun goes down. This was intentional. I need this journal to be found. If things get bad, I will bury this journal so it can be found one day. I can't risk having the ash people find it and destroy it.

I might be going crazy here – actually, I KNOW I

am – but I need to get rid of the village. What if I tried to set the dragon free? Would it know I was helping and let me ride it off into the sky like the Luckdragon in *The Neverending Story*? Or would it know the difference and decapitate me with a single bite? Probably the latter. Maybe just getting rid of any trace of this village, including the dragon, is necessary. I just need to get the hell out and go somewhere very far away. That was my plan in the first place, now I just need to fucking do it.

September 5, 1998

This will be the last diary entry. I'm going to bury this journal and if you find it, I'm either dead or I left and I'm very, very far away. Tonight, I'm going to attempt to free the dragon. No living thing should have to burn bodies in order to stay alive. Still not sure if it's alive, but if it is, I'm going to either free it or kill it and put it out of its misery.

I was able to grab a gas can from the corner of the barn next to the one I'm staying in. There's a little bit of gas inside and I'm going to throw it into the stove when the body-transporters leave. That's when the fire is at its largest and it'll light up the shed more quickly. If I die in the inferno, please treat this as a possibly insane testimony regarding the events soon to ensue.

GOD SPEED!

Nothing else was written after this last entry. The village had been burned to the ground. No source of the fire has been found or determined.

CROSSFIRE

BY ASHLEY DIOSES

Beneath the stone, I was
	awakened at long last
Away from towns and farmers
	from which I was cast.
From under darksome caverns
	where I started out,
I prowled the woods as fae
	abandoned the route.

I spread my wings and leaped into
	the autumn air.
The birds then ceased to sing
	while I flew without care.
A hunger rose inside of me yet all
	prey vanished;
My cunning prey often could
	sense when I was famished.

One lone yet knightly creature, of
	a beauty rare,

Appeared across the glade and
        then she seemed to dare
Me with her shiny, spiral horn and
        hide of white;
The unicorn would make such a
        delicious bite.

I followed her atop a hill where
        she stood strong.
She mocked my majesty but
        would not for too long.
I dove in for the kill but as I drew
        so near
I sensed a beast, another predator
        was here.

Another dragon came from
        opposite the hill;
He also flew in towards the exact
        same kill.
We dove, then nearly collided and
        almost crashed.
We quickly avoided each other yet
        tails thrashed.

We clawed and bit as we both
        soared through the bright sky
For the new challenger and prey
        would need to die.
Our voices roared and fire was
        spit, both our tails slashed
As we cut through the air with
        reddened flames that flashed.

Emeralds and amaranthine hues
    bedecked our scales
Yet sharpened talons could pierce
    the strongest mail.
Our muscles ached and bones
    became so weak and broken
And yet when it was over, there
    was no more token.

The unicorn was gone, for she left
    in a hurry
While I was locked in brutal
    combat with my quarry.
I raided through the grove yet I
    began to tire.
I left my prey who vanished from
    our fierce crossfire.

DRAGONSPEAK

BY ASHLEY DIOSES

Her scales of molten gold
Lit up the stormy skies.
Her teeth of winter's cold
Were quick to silence cries.

Her eyes were precious stones,
The coldest of sapphires.
They matched the Reaper's
    throne
Of bones, pale as vampires.

Her dragonspeak took toll.
Her voice of thunder's kiss
Has singed the very soul,
Seared skin with fire's hot hiss.

Her claws were swords to play
Against their crafted steel.
She is the one to slay;
When will they ever kneel?

She, goddess of the flame,
Harbinger of fierce pain,
Arises to her claim
Of heavens, and the slain.

YOUNG RITA

BY CHRISTOPHER LESKO

HER ALCOHOLIC PARENTS wanted to name her Margarita. The judge wouldn't let them. They settled on Rita. She was the only one named Rita in her school, and kids picked on her for having an old lady's name. They picked on her for a lot of things. Her parents picked on her even more.

Most mornings her mother stomped up the stairs, into Rita's bedroom, and poked her with the handle-end of a wooden broom. "Wake up for makeup," she'd shout over and over until Rita rolled out of bed, or she would drag Rita out of bed by her feet. Either way, she forced Rita to the chair in front of her grandma's vanity hutch.

Most of the old junk went to Goodwill after her grandma's death, but that piece of furniture was about the nicest thing she had. All cherry oak. Heavy as hell. Rita remembered her dad and her uncle Mark almost broke their backs hauling it up the stairs. They drank a lot of beer afterward. She remembered that because they were drunk as fuck when they tricked her into guzzling Castrol motor oil that she thought was a beer.

It began one early morning while mother was brushing Rita's hair. Rita sat in front of the vanity mirror staring at her own reflection. She imagined diving into her pupil, an outer space portal where she could swim for eternity as a mermaid constellation, anything to escape the torture of her mother's morning routine for her.

"You have hair like your grandma," her mother said, raking the comb across Rita's scalp. She referred to Rita's thinning hair. Over the years, her mother had ripped most of it out by combing it the awful way she did. And over the years, her mother's tender face disappeared. Replaced with a pall of black smoke was how Rita began to see it.

"You're hurting me."

"Am not."

"Are too."

"Hold still and quit being a fuckin' baby. You're almost eighteen-years-old for God's sake. Act like it." Her grasp below the jaw clenched Rita's cheeks.

If Rita cried, her mother would scold her for it—she always wanted her to stop being a baby. So as Rita's eyes began to pool, her vision turning fuzzy, she imagined herself sinking to the bottom of a murky pond where she could bury herself in the mud at the bottom.

"Did you hear what I said?"

Rita didn't know what was said. She didn't care.

"I said you look pretty."

Rita ignored her.

"Can I have a smile?" her mother asked gently.

Rita didn't want to fucking smile.

"Smile," her mother growled with a sound deep from the hell within her.

She thought Rita shook her head no—but Rita's head just did that kind of thing when she was frightened —so the handle-end of the broom speared Rita on all sides, knocking her to the floor while always managing to avoid her face. The day her mother would accidentally hit her in the temple and kill her couldn't come soon enough, Rita always thought.

Against her mightiest attempt to hold it all back, the levee broke. Rita cried so hard she couldn't even breathe and wished she wasn't crying because it hurt her sides to cry. She wiped tears in her nightgown and was reminded of her grandma in the same nightgown she wore all day, every day for the last few years of her life. And how she once saw her mother helping her grandma to the bathroom and it looked like she had bed sores all over her body, but they were probably welts from her mother beating her too.

"C'mon. Quit overreacting you little drama queen. I didn't hit you that hard. Get up." The broom handle dug into place under Rita's leg as a wedge to lift her. "Get up."

Choking down tears, Rita pulled herself up onto the chair in front of the vanity; time for makeup.

Her mother popped the cap off the candy apple red lipstick and smeared it all over Rita's cheeks, totally missing her lips. "You look pretty."

Rita did not look pretty at all. Her mother was either

high on dope or drunk or both and just wanted to be funny.

"Smile."

This time Rita smiled: a chainsaw blade of jagged teeth. She hated her teeth.

"You need braces," her mother said. Rita didn't know why she said that. They'd been through it before. Rita told her she wanted them. But her mother would never get them for her. Always blew her money on drugs instead. Rita was old enough now to know what "China White" really was. She'd tried some. Her mother didn't know she tried it, but she did. It was hers. Rita stole it. It helped the pain go away, helped her sleep at night, and helped her not to cry like a baby.

"I packed you Little Debbie's in your lunch today."

So what? Mother packed them every day. She didn't know why she was trying to be sweet now. Maybe it was because she felt sorry for hurting her. Doubtful. It was Saturday, though; no school. Yes, indeed her mother was intoxicated. Rita needed to get away.

«

She'd partied at the Scottish Inn on Market Street over a dozen times with other kids in her grade. They were not the friends she usually hung out with, but she liked whenever they invited her because they were funnier and more exciting than her friends who just wanted to go to the movies and hang out at Steak n' Shake every weekend. If Amber tried a new flavor milkshake it was like holy shit, look out, she's getting wild, ya'll. The Scottish Inn wasn't nothing fancy. Thirty-two dollars a night. It had the same white and green coat of paint since it opened back in the 70s. Rooms mostly occupied by truckers. The last time Rita partied there was a blast. Seven of her friends packed in a single room: Rita, two other girls, Chuck and four other guys. They passed around a can of Dust Off, careful not to fill their lungs with too much of the shit. They also had a bottle of 151 mixed with cans of cherry cola, and that night Rita smoked a bong for the first time. Damn, that thing ripped her good. She never laughed so hard about whatever it was. It felt good for her to laugh and good to feel cooler than her geeky Steak N' Shake friends. This time going to the Scottish Inn, however, it was just going to be her and Chuck; alone at last again.

Chuck sat in a white plastic chair out front of the motel room smoking a cigarette. Rita liked how he looked good in his tight black jeans, cowboy boots, and white v-neck. He wore his thin gold necklace she had stolen for him from the jewel case at Walmart. Chuck knew how to treat Rita right: he could make her feel sexy. Rita hoped it would turn into love. But at the time, it was pure fun. She brought him the powder and he bought her CD's and ice cream. A Dairy Queen they always went to was a stone's throw away from the motel. After she planted a smooch on Chuck, his face lit up with a big smile. Rita hoped he had that CD she asked him for.

"I gotta a surprise for you," Chuck said. He ran his thumb across his lips to wipe them dry.

"Yeah? What is it?" She didn't see anything around other than his pack of smokes. She didn't want those.

"It's a surprise."

Well, since he was going to be like that, Rita pretended she didn't care about his surprise anymore.

She walked to the rose bushes out front by the entrance sign. She looked back to see if he watched her. He did. Then he stood and grabbed his smokes. She could smell the red roses without even having to lean in. The sun cast an orange glow over everything, a couple hours away from setting. Chuck met her by the rose bushes.

"Smells nice," he said.

"Sure does." Rita noticed the dirt all dried up in the flower bed and that people had smothered their cigarette butts in it.

"So did you get me my CD?"

"It's in my car. I'll bring it in when we get back."

Chuck and Rita headed over to the Dairy Queen. Tina was working. Rita knew Tina from school. Tina had nice tits. Big ones Rita wished she had. She's told Rita she lets guys suck them in the movie theater. Rita could never do something like that in public. Tina knew what Rita and Chuck did alone at the motel though, Rita had told her. Tina was cool. She'd never gossip.

Chuck got a vanilla cake cone. He looked like such a doofus licking it. His tongue hung out as he spun the cone really fast. He'd lap up drips like a dog. And once the ice cream had diminished enough he'd put his whole mouth over the top and suck with slurping noises. Rita ordered the same thing every time. It was what she needed to open her third eye: a cookies n' cream ice cream cone, sugar cone. Once her third eye opened, it was easier to take in everything else that usually came next back at the motel room.

It's 6:66 pm. Mother is going to kill me. I'm late for dinner.
Ha!

. . .

It's 6:67 pm. Mother is going to kill me. But I love my Imagine Dragons' CD. I feel thunder.
Ha!

It's 6:68 pm. Mother is going to kill me. No, she won't, she's probably wasted like me.
Ha!

It's 6:69 pm. Mother is going to kill me. I'm all out of the sexy stuff.
Ha!

It's 6:70 pm. Mother is going to kill me. I need more.
Ha!

It's 6:71 pm. Mother is going to kill me. This CD will work better if I crush it up and snort it.
Ha!

It's 6:72 pm. Mother is going to kill me. I can't feel my nose. It appears missing.
Ha!

«

Mr. Carter woke Rita on the front porch of his house the next morning. Slumped over, right at the foot of her neighbor's front door, she laid with her house key in hand.

"You're going to get treatment," he said in a somber voice.

"What do you mean?" Rita moaned.

"I mean I have someone coming to take you there … to a treatment center."

"Why me?" Rita lit up. "It's my parents' fault. They fucked me up. Someone needs to lock them up!"

Mr. Carter offered his hand, but she picked herself up and stepped off his front porch, headed to her own house. She needed her nightgown. She needed her bed. She needed to wake up again where everything would be fine.

"Rita, please. We don't want to lose you. You're too young to be throwing your life away," Mr. Carter pleaded.

"I'm not an addict! Mind your own fucking business!"

The screen door to her house was broken; stayed half-open all the time. She unlocked the storm door and ran up to her room. She didn't hear anyone yell at her so she suspected no one was home. Safe and sound, she fell fast asleep.

Rita wished it happened like that.

Before she made it back to her house, a police car pulled into her driveway. Rita knew what they were to do with her. She didn't want to make it worse. She did as they said.

They took her to rehab and she hated them for it. But there she was allowed to cry all she wanted: *I wish they would have just taken me to jail. I don't need this. What are they trying to do to me? Make me hate myself even more? I'm too young for this. It's going to be my birthday next week and I don't*

want to spend it locked up in here. Just let me live a little more
before you take it all away. Why now?

That night, resting with a bucket next to her bed in the room, Rita heard a voice call out to her by name. A gentle voice, one she never listened to before. She sat up. Then she heard it say "Trust me." And those words made her feel like a newborn baby in the arms of its loving parents. Tears of sorrow she felt for being in rehab and for never listening to the voice before soaked her pillow.

Rita didn't have to say it aloud but wanted to. "I am listening," she replied. At that moment, all the drugs in her system, the hate she felt toward herself and her parents and the whole unfair world flushed away.

IN THE NIGHT WE TURN CONSUMED BY DRAGONS

BY FIONA MAEVE GEIST

(In girum imus nocte et consumimur igni)

Handsome Hank, heretic of the Hunk of Burning Love, lies gasping on the floor. The venom flows freely through his veins. He vomits up something with the consistency of coffee grounds, the color of Cheerwine; his lips turn blue. He stops shaking and starts cooling. The snake priestess flicks her forked tongue enticingly; her chainmail bikini provides endless vulnerable, exposed points to attack. Her barbed whip swishes along the ground waiting to dart up again with a sundering crack.

. . .

It is hazy under the soft incandescent deck light unfocused across the back yard. Andrew's hands shake as he lights a cigarette. The back-porch door slides open and Nick bursts out—a blur of manic, unfocused energy. Already his hands are dancing along with his stream of consciousness like a pair of lilting birds.

"Dude, that was fucking great that was like fucking something that would be airbrushed on a van..." he shakes a black pack of cigarettes despondently. "Hey, bum me one of yours? I'll pay you back tomorrow?"

Andrew obligingly shakes a red soft pack at Nick. Nick pulls an exaggerated face along with the proffered cigarette.

"Fucking cowboy killers? You know you aren't gonna live forever smoking that trash!"

Andrew sneers "Any smokes will kill you, but those hippie organic ones will make you feel like it," he slouches against the wall and sighs. "Still... anything is better than we used to steal your mother's scrawny bitch cigarettes that were all menthol and paper..." he trails off. "Still, those were the golden years... we first started playing—with a bunch of pewter figures and green army men in your basement."

Nick exhales smoke upwards and it looks suspended in the light. "Y'know... we didn't really play, I mean yes you memorized the rules and were a little bitch about it but we never killed no fucking dragon."

Andrew giggles until he starts coughing. "You went away to college and came back *all fucked up*, and you still haven't learned to talk like you don't fuck your cousin—"

"One, it's weird enough that my cousin dances at the Bull and *two*." Nick pokes Andrew in the chest for emphasis. "I've seen my cousin dance when I took Tim out for a lap dance during fall break—which let me fucking tell you: there is no way in hell I would fuck my weirdass cousin."

Andrew awkwardly hugs Nick around the head. "I love you man, since we were fucking kids and shit, but the fact you didn't *leave a goddamn strip club* while your *blood relative* was jerking off truckers in sweatpants makes you the most white-trash motherfucker I have ever fucking met."

Nick adopts a simpering affect. "I do *declare* that you are no gentleman, Andrew Overholt." His voice returns to normal. "And you are dodging the issue that we never bagged a dragon."

Andrew tries to interject but Nick isn't speaking with gaps in his words. Andrew lights his cigarette as Nick rapidly continues. "We bagged a manticore, dragon men, lizardmen, and a sexy lady face on a snake with six rows of massive titties you fucking *sexual deviant*." Nick emphasizes the words in the shrillest tone he can manage. "So, we know you have some fucking issues with your dad or whatever but that is neither here nor there." His eyes shine with energized focus. "This summer, I'm gonna kill a dragon… anything to not fixate on how you wanna be whipped by snake women. Which, by the way, I am sure at least one of my cousin's cracked-out friends has some snake scale pattern tattoos and a split tongue… you want me to hook you up I can call Charlene up on her mobile. She may even sell us some weed."

Andrew shrugs as if Nick's words piled up like a car crash designed by Rube Goldberg and only now he can slough them off his shoulders. "Nick, I know you like to get all the fuck ahead of yourself but *why* did you go home for fall break and not tell me, and *why* would you take Tim to a strip club?" His voice warps from mildly hurt to perplexed.

Nicks hand darts out in supplication and Andrew shakes him another cigarette. Nick lights it while twirling as he takes the first drag; Andrew adopts his slouch against the wall.

"Well," Nick continues in a more serious tone, "you were having so much fun at college and decided to go so far away cause you're ashamed of us knowing no matter what you got on the SATs you are still the uncool loser who never got fucked in high school and was all fucking maladjusted listening to metal made by Nazi zombies. Anyway, I was close to home and Tim and Brandon had both come up to visit me—by the way, Brandon fucking enlisted, he's a full on fucking babykiller, we get to spit on him when he comes back and ask him how much blood he spilled for oil; it's gonna be dope as hell."

The rapid stucco of words almost suffocates the meaning, the spaces between them razor thin. "So, I went back and Brandon signed his contract to go bring our disobedient serfs to fucking heel and Tim's acne cleared up and he apparently got self-esteem and instead of doing drugs like normal, god-fearing Americans should, he instead starts hitting the gym and gets recruited to be a male stripper." Nick lets up to clock Andrew's disbelief before plowing ahead, undaunted. "Like, whatever gay dudes there are around here and a bunch of moms and spinsters pay money to stare at Tim's—apparently massive—dick. Like get slapped in the face with it; I don't really know he doesn't talk about it but he has nice clothes and a car and an apartment and isn't crashing in his remarried dad's guest room so he's smarter than us stupid fuckers with our one year of college down."

Andrew spits and looks at the horizon as if it has some convenient answer.

"Oh, one last thing," Nick continues, "Tim is like mad sensitive about it—so don't talk about it when he comes to play next week, he'll probably brag about it but who fucking knows what goes on in his head? But anyway, we got drunk, Tim told us, and Brandon and I decided he should see how the other half lives... well, strips...." Nick looks at the filter to the spent cigarette expectantly until Andrew shakes another one to him. "ANYWAY," Nick takes a deep breath, "that's how we wound up in the fucking strip club while my cousin was dancing and I was too drunk to drive and Brandon and Tim weren't much better and Charlene—well she made us call her Ruby which is dumb as all fucking hell because she already had a goddamn stripper name— talked to the owner and we got half price beers and didn't get ID'd. Anyway, Brandon can't play because he is defending our freedoms from Islam or something gay like that and Tim had to work a bachelorette party, but next week he and Holly are gonna show up so my dumb ass won't get killed and we can play for longer and not have to watch Cheaters."

Andrew smiles, edges slowly creeping up. It would be nearly imperceptible if it didn't angle his cigarette upwards. "Yeah man, it'll be dope next week. I'm like, reading and I've got some ideas and shit. You're still weird as all hell Nick, never fucking change."

"Yeah, you and your fucking cowboy killers aren't gonna change anytime soon."

"Heh, didn't you have to take some sort of sensitivity class in college?" Andrew asks as Nick walks towards his car hands jangling in his pockets.

"I don't remember," Nick shouts, cupping his hands around his mouth and being rewarded with a rejoinder of barking dogs, "if I did it probably didn't stick because

I was too busy getting laid and being fuckin' awesome!" Nick bows and flips Andrew off before hopping into his beater.

Andrew lights another cigarette and slumps against the wall.

Poncho, master of the bongo drum, is peppered with primitive crossbow bolts as the cacophonous hissing of the lizard men buzzes from the undergrowth. Scarlet Rachel and Happy Harry Hardon recruit Denver Max from the conveniently proximate tavern and return to the jungle—hacking their way through the blasphemous cries of lizardmen—delving deep into the inverted ziggurat. The heads on stakes and cauldrons overflowing with viscera and bones do not deter their murderous search for the Golden Idol of the Dread Armies of Night.

The floodlights are still on in the gas station parking lot. The station itself was torn down and paved over and now the lights illuminate nothing but cracked asphalt and endless blankets of mosquitoes and moths crashing ceaselessly into the lights, their corpses fluttering down limp and broken. Nick and Andrew sit on the cooling car hood and stare into the upturned lights that eat the stars.

"Y'know…," Nick drawls, his voice hazy and half slurred from the icy slush and sweetened artificial color amended with pilfered white wine, "our characters are a lot like those moths?"

Andrew looks perplexed. "You think a fake dude in a conquistador helmet smashing lizard dudes with a claymore is like a bunch of fucking moths? You get high without telling me?"

Nick lets out an exaggerated sigh and starts rambling

through his train of thought. "Nah, like metaphorically, right? Like… those lights are big shining things that drag the doomed bugs to it and you tell us where treasure is and our goal is to accrue treasure and then murder us when we fuck up looting stuff." Nick spits off the side of the car and shakes his cigarette pack, tapping one into his mouth and offering another to Andrew. He lights both with an exaggerated flourish of his zippo.

"Nick…" Andrew drawls with a laconic burble, "you're getting weird again. Like, the game would be boring as hell if you played normal, well-adjusted people… you wouldn't do shit but work at a store and have kids or whatever… and no one would want to play that unless they were seriously impaired… y'know?"

Nick considers the viewpoint, chewing his filter as the cherry inches closer to it.

Finally, he responds. "No, but like… the game implies we will traipse through some dungeons and kill dragons, not 'be shot apart by gross lizard dudes and have our heads stuck on spears'—like, dude, you are a sick fuck—it's less piles of treasure and more 'random stuff I pilfered from the cell of a lizard priest whose face I bashed in with a claymore.' And to be fair, Happy Harry is a fuckbeast who lives to hear the lamentation of his enemies' women—are there lady lizardmen? But seriously, he's like desecrating temples to pluck gems and flaked-off gold to go sell to merchants."

"Sure, Nick," Andrew says with a somewhat patronizing tone, "I could just give you scads of loot and you could have optimum gear and it would be boring. Like… it's like a rich kid slumming it by hitting the rails and going to punk shows? Like, that shit is dumb as hell."

Nick lights another cigarette and passes it to Andrew before lighting one for himself. "Ok, I see this touched a nerve and I'm not your therapist and yeah without challenge the game would be dumb, but why are we playing in such a grime-and-dysentery scenario rather than dashing in with flashing swords like in those movies that are way too fucking long?"

Andrew makes a sour face. "Because that shit is *boring* Nick; have you read those books since growing up? Their universe is fucking stupid: elves are effete dicks and dwarves are stodgy dicks and some fucker sings some stupid fucking song while a forgetful old man rambles on about fucking history. It's like a marginally less depressing version of visiting my grandpa when the Alzheimer's got real fucking bad."

Nick giggles, "Jesus, we are real fucked up, aren't we?"

Andrew lets out a weak laugh. "Yeah, let's go to the bodega and get some snacks. I'll treat—since you object so heavily to being a syphilitic degenerate grubbing around for wealth and wanna be a prince."

Nick snaps his fingers. "That's it! Fucking adventurers, man, they're like that goddamn show where people loot storage lockers and sell random junk at flea markets! They're fucking weirdo scumfucks like that, aren't they? Also—lemme give this to you straight no fucking chaser —Happy Harry wraps his shit; he is not losing any fucking loot he takes from his victims... err enemies... to fucking child support... fuck no."

Andrew guffaws. "Nick, you fucking degenerate, what the fuck is he gonna wrap it with, a fucking beaver pelt?"

Nick flicks his cigarette into the night sky. "I don't fucking know," he interjects in a slightly petulant tone.

Andrew ruffles his hair and stares out into the distance. "I'm just giving you shit; thanks for suggesting we do this and recruiting Holly and Tim—it was cool to see them."

"Yeah, maybe don't be such a fucking stranger; running off to a big city and forgetting your friends. Like, fuck, man it was kinda shitty you just vanished?" Nick's voice wavers.

Andrew shakes a cigarette out of his soft pack and lights it before crumpling the empty pack and throwing it away. Nick lightly punches him in the shoulder "bro, you had fucking cigarettes and you took mine! Shit, if this is your treat get me a pack? And some fucking chips!"

Andrew rolls his eyes. "It's nice to know you never change—and you still never hit me back for the cigarettes last week."

Nick lights his own. "No one really changes—other than Tim—dude has self-esteem and gets pussy on the regular and isn't moon eyed over my fucked-up cousin."

"Who you watched strip… with your two buddies from high school," Andrew interjects.

"Yeah, yeah give me shit about it… I looked away when she was on stage and—minus her dancing—it was a pretty fun time, y'know?"

"Yeah." Andrew rolls off the hood. "C'mon, life ain't getting any more vibrant in this fucking parking lot talking about feelings."

Nick rolls off and they roll away. The tires kick up dust and discarded cigarette packs, crunching the occasional discarded beer can. The car shakes from the metal in the CD player.

Scarlet Rachel convulses wildly as her stomach expands and squirms, finally bursting open like an overripe peach. Parasitic worms writhe about, spilling forth from the wound. Happy Harry

Hardon and Denver Max rapidly douse her body and most of the room in lamp oil and hit it with a Molotov. Their lantern-bearer (now named Princess Bathory) receives a battlefield promotion. It is Princess Bathory who eventually catches the wizard. The wizard eventually expires under the prolonged enhanced interrogation techniques, finally giving away the location before succumbing to his wounds in utter agony. Denver and Harry are disinclined to spend the loot they have acquired from his home to 'resurrect him and torture his bitch ass to death again,' as suggested by Princess Bathory. Denver learns forbidden magic from the grimoire bound in tattooed human flesh.

Andrew is lighting his cigarette as he steps out of the sliding door—Holly and Nick are already outside laughing uproariously.

Nicks' hands are a blur as he effusively praises Holly. "That shit was *inspired,* like, what the *everliving fuck* is wrong with you girl? You're a really twisted sister and shit."

Holly spits into the misting almost rain. "No, I'm not! That wizard *had it coming!*"

Andrew breathes out smoke incredulously as a retort. "C'mon, you can't seriously believe that doesn't stop you from being lawful good?!"

"I don't know? Maybe because there isn't a Genova Convention concerning fucking monsters?" Holly smirks in reply.

"Ok," Andrew sighs exaggeratedly, "but you nailed a man's face to the floor and set him on fire…"

"Which was fucking awesome!" Nick shrieks.

"…After ripping out his fingernails," Andrew continues, scowling at Nick.

"Did the Wizard get consent to harvest that human

flesh his spells were bound in?" Holly interrupts. "Is it ethically fucking sourced?"

Andrew pouts and despondently lights another cigarette. "How is that relevant? Like, it's morally uncomplicated to kill him but torturing him is another thing entirely..." he fakes a shudder. "That was fucking *dark*."

Everyone stares blankly until Andrew starts giggling. "Really? You thought I was offended you tortured some wizard with the Necronomicon? Fucking whatever; now Tim can consort with dark powers."

"Are we supposed to care about the morality of stuff? Like, are we failing some morality test by being creepy, murderous drifters?"

"There was an evangelical version? Like, how the weird kids who prayed at the flag had their own version of normal-people bands," Holly responds animatedly, "like, there was this stupid as fuck game where you had to quote the Bible to do magic and you couldn't die?"

Andrew and Nick seem perplexed.

"Like, reject sodomy and stone your children to death and you get to cast a spell," She strikes a melo-dramatic wizarding pose. "But fucking seriously, imagine thinking the devil made dinosaur bones to fuck with your head, listening to some shitty Christian metal, having a shitty haircut your mom gave you and not getting to fuck until you are married... then you get an endless cycle of pregnancy." Holly crinkles her face.

"Evangelicals just do a bunch of hand stuff," Nick offers, with a wink.

Andrew snorts. "How would you fucking know? You cried your whole relationship with Alison because you couldn't get any and 'were as bad off as your stupid, unfuckable dick'... why did you date that weirdo for months?"

Nick mumbles something.

"Huh? What was that?"

"I thought she'd do anal, since Jesus freaks just save their pussy for marriage, and I figured if it sucked I'd tell her I couldn't be attracted to an immodest woman and if it was good I could have weird religious sex on the regular and not have to worry about pregnancy, which is fucking dope."

"Nick, you fucking deviant, those fucking kids have comics about how if you wear a 'No Fear' shirt you will commit suicide to prove you are hardcore and that a secret cabal of Satanists are why Andrew's mom left his dad for another woman," Holly shrieked, "and you think that Jesus freak weirdo who smelled like baking soda and probably had never seen a razor was going to let you fuck her up the ass? You honestly believed that? You went to fucking weird megachurch Hitler Youth style rallies against abortion and did bible study and partook in their weird fucking pyramid scheme-exploiting, cousin-fucking white trash lifestyle on the hope you could fuck her ass?"

"... and then you didn't even get that—just stupid dopey Christian shit. And you had the goddamned nerve to call me a fucking bitch in high school when you degraded yourself so shamelessly for the hope of fucking some weird girl in the brown?" Andrew exclaims, incredulous.

"Look, some of that stuff was funny as hell, like when they had Christian pro wrestling and there was free soda and pizza and I was like... this close," he holds his fingers a millimeter apart, "to tearing that ass apart."

"No, no, no. You went to some dork ass Christian

shit you don't get to pull a fast one and be like 'oh this? It was *ironic*, I wasn't really a desperate bitch—I swear.'" Holly rolls her eyes.

"Seriously, you don't get to dodge how humiliating that should be—you willingly hung out with *Christians* in a desperate ploy to get laid, you fucking heathen motherfucker."

"Whatever, fuck you both—fuck you both with Tim's monster treeroot of a dick"

"You know, for an alleged heterosexual, you think a lot about Tim's massive hog."

"Whatever. Want me to prove my heterosexuality? I'll totally fuck you right now, Holly!"

"Bruh, you praised the Lord… even Brandon's Susie Rotten-Crotch girl who gets plowed by everyone wouldn't fuck you… you may have to go to one of those weird churches where they marry everyone at random."

The bickering continues until the dawn nullifies the glow of the exterior lights. They pile into Nick's car to buy soda and cigarettes and crash in Andrew's basement upon their return. Eventually succumbing to inertia and exhaustion, the conversation ceases.

The party slaughters its way through lizardmen, wizards, a manti-core… they venture deep into the earth and they slaughter the skulking cannibals who cling to the darkness. They go mad, and begin to starve. They eat a henchman and see daylight. Nick insists that cannibalism is a neutral good action because it isn't wasteful—also, that, by extension, killing is never evil as it is necessary for biological processes. Tim apparently had done some math on this since all that is on TV when he is off work are nature documentaries and poor people screaming and punching…. Time wears on. *They acquire wealth beyond measure and magic beyond understanding. Still, they seek the dragon. They have built this trail of bones; none of the original party remained, only the singular burning focus on the dragon.* Andrew drew it out, sometimes because he had trouble staying focused, sometimes because Nick's laser-like focus strayed to some peripheral concern and he could not let it go. *Still, they hacked forward trading blood for gold, gold for iron, iron spilled blood and the gold trailed in its wake.*

Handsome Dick Manitoba, Solid Gold Princess and Denver Max clone 3—the whole cloning thing became so complex and weird—*stand upon the bedrock of creation facing down ΒΑΒΥΛΩΝ, Mother of Dragons and Serpentine Abominations. She whose breath spreads famine and calamity. She whose wings stirring is the herald of whirlwinds. Ruler of the First City of Men, site of every treasure.*

"Fuck, ok I need a smoke before I do this," Nick interjects.

"Before *YOU* do this? Ex-Fucking-Scuse yourself Nick, because Denver-Fucking-Max III is about to make that bitch of a dragon eat his spells... also, give me one of your stupid fucking organic cigarettes for slandering Denver like that."

Nick taps out a cigarette and contemptuously flings it at Tim

"You're both delusional; Solid Gold Princess is clearly the only one saving you both from certain death at the hands of your own incompetence."

"Oh, of course, how could we forget, you are so insecure you *need* your character to be a princess to prove that you're a girl."

"Ok, fuck you Nick, you owe me a fucking cigarette!"

A second cigarette is absently flung to Holly and Nick dramatically tramps out where Andrew already has his hoodie scrunched about him, shivering slightly as he smokes his cigarette.

"The dragon good enough for you, Nick? Wanted to be sure you bagged a worthy dragon…"

"Nah, I know you think you can kill me, but you can't keep a fucking good man down…"

"Oh because good men, that's a thing that's real…" Holly remarks sarcastically.

"You know you're a dyke, right Holly? Like, you know how I know you're a dyke?"

"Because clearly any woman who has turned you down is a dyke?"

"Because you hate men—Jesus, why do you think it is so complicated—your problem is you also hate women, which makes you…"

"A crazy cat lady? Still better than if I let your broken dog dick spit a fucking child in me which—let me remind you—is what you wanted to do, because, and I quote, 'There don't have to be feelings, just me rawing you in your pussy like I'm going to get you pregnant,' because you really know how to sell anyone on sex with your stupid ass. Also, if I was gonna fuck any of you, it would be Tim since he has a monster dick and a nice car he can fingerblast me in"

Nick winces, "Fucking gross"

"That would probably spoil the interior—also Nick, have you ever been laid?" Tim sighed.

"You know there used to be a signature dragon?" Andrew interjects, seemingly at random.

"What?"

"The game—there used to be *a dragon,* singular, not *dragons,* plural, and the dragon fucking sucked? It was an ineffective Saturday Morning Cartoon Villain and pulled stupid pranks and whined and acted like an asshole—you know they wanted kids to play these games?"

"Yeah, because when Nick was **not** plowing Alison in the ass, they gave him one of those comics about how you worship Satan by doing this and how you are gonna convert us into a lesbian coven with your mom and her yoga teacher."

"Thanks Holly, please bring my muff-diving Mom into this shit. *ANYWAY*, there is one dragon. This is the only dragon left. The last dragon. And you're going to try to kill it—like you are torching actual history and then looting it like some fucking Vandals."

"Dope, I get to destroy fucking history... also is this dragon a hoarder?" Nick's enthusiasm quickly became quizzical, "like, why does this dragon have so much of recorded history lying around? Is this like *Grey Gardens*? Is this dragon just tottering around a decaying mansion remembering history and drinking tea?"

"Nick... are you fucking serious? Like, are you a spastic? This is an eons-spanning dragon that was there at the birth of creation and your question is 'is the dragon sundowning like in that depressing documentary?'—which we watched because you were too stoned to operate the remote, I might add! Because you are a lightweight bitch." Andrews tone is placid in spite of his irritation.

"Both of you shut up or I'm gonna let Tim wreck my ass in your depressing basement. But seriously, are dragons hoarders? Are the heroes just like... social workers who go murder them and stop their hoard pile?"

"Holly, I would never fuck you—even with Andrews unfuckable cock—but basically, you want to make this one of those games about feelings, which is absolutely uncool? Because if you wanna be uncool, I can go get laid or something…"

"Shut the fuck up Tim; fucking the dust out of lonely women sloshed on Long Island Iced Tea doesn't make you cool, it makes you a vector for HPV. Anyway, I wanna know because Nick brought up an interesting point: are we just murderous drifters killing a decrepit old dragon for her stuff…"

"Holly, reality check: the dragon is ancient, it isn't decrepit. Like the pyramids and stuff that just persists. The dragon is eternal and powerful and not sundowning…" Andrew adds sourly.

Holly sighs. "You don't need to overcompensate with your dragon! Jesus bro, ease the fuck up! We will take you to the strip club later and Nick can pretend to not enviously watch you while Charlene rides your dick."

"Gross, ok I'm murdering this fucking dragon and I am not going to watch my cousin dance."

"Yes you will, because you's a bitch and this will be mad fun and Andrew will stop looking exasperated all the fucking time because he needs to get fucking laid and almost everyone you know fucked your cousin anyway *and* it's a nicer bar, and they don't card us, and I can brag about my money and my monster dick and throw cash around. Still probably won't get laid but whatever; I can tell them about slaying a dragon and it'll be cool?" Tim himself seems confused by the extent of his sudden outburst.

"Tim… what do women talk to you about?"

"Nothing as cool as killing a fucking dragon… mostly just small talk anyway? Like, it's admirable: everyone knows their role, I pretend to be interested and get paid and they can talk about whatever they want and it costs less than therapy, so after we kill this dragon, I'll drop a couple stacks on you fucking losers. Holly can admit she wants to eat some pussy, and everyone working gets a bunch of cash."

"Ok, fucking sold—thanks for spotting me," Nick enthuses.

"You know I'm not a lesbian right…?"

Nick giggles. "Shut up Holly. We've accepted your sapphic tendencies; you just need to be honest with yourself."

"*Whatever*, I'm going to smash a fucking dragon—Andrew are you fucking coming?" Holly remarks, striding in.

"Yeah, gimme a second to finish my smoke I'll be right in."

"You know you're a fucking idiot, right Nick?"

"Shut the fuck up and spot me a cowboy killer before I go wreck this dragon."

The last cigarette is tapped from the pack. The pack crumpled into Andrew's pocket. Shortly after, the door slides open and they enter.

And so in the darkest depths of the earth, they came upon the dragon as old as time, powerful as a god and they stood on the precipice of eternity.

IMPACTED SUPPLEMENTATION

BY DAV CRABES

THINGS HAVE CHANGED. I'm in Asia, sprawled before a video in some strange study; Italian mock-superiority, some ticking things; children of Cantonese origin, retro soundtrack. Still-born waves of awakening, as errands pile up around fruiting bodies.

Some near-art discharge forms curious identity; blood-scented, eyes like radiators, sporting a stream of focused fuck-taint and a desperate need for justice.

I feel malevolence towards this curiosity / this steel lipped charmer / this evil, looming wolf. He hands me a case, and with his shocking frame undertaking magical

Mexican part-shits, dissolves into the TV, voice splintering into static.

"Rend her years, you morbid stalker!"

Even when earned, it's barely in and it's out already; I honor the wall and exit north with an abrupt stench of sudden prestige.

***People suffering; famine in the background.**

I rode past in compliance, moist with self-satisfaction, inspiring nothing but wonder in those viewing my motions / structure; one important reeb is stating its amour using lithenic ointment and 16th century verse.

"I'm embroidering; breastfeeding."

Rising in reaction to the bitch, inhaling diseased dreams from a Chinese puzzle-box packed with prolintanone, eager to navigate, to release our solids, to **adhere** to; repetition clinging to early exposure and separate fears.

Cohesion is cured like sickness, and we slide into truth tilting madness; it offers change, temporary insight, and some kind of lifestyle. Bloody precursors fatigued by ill definitions, diseased impulsivity, and problem grammar based on quickly clotting curds of humor.

We drift about, abnormal and wasted; crooked, dry and malnourished (because it relates to life). Translating kun-system visions while other plot elements undermine the theme or just do harm.

Mating without scope or template / with the veracity of urine, my death-step negates the wank massive. One noted graduate burst under pressure with the statutory anguish of a voluptuous hemorrhoid.

Months sank chasing that blue Kenyan devil, cloud stalking / keeping track, while some half-Polish child screens intimate videos of my well structured cousin; its drifting matter and stifling descriptions cause an outbreak, and then things get gone.

After joining ourselves in situ, the gunman bent over, opened his gelatinous anus, and made commence on his curious quest, birthing non-stop in his chewed quarters.

and it is worthwhile to note that they have to spend some time / spend the rest of the day, to get the trophies of death.

"You may not reside in Auschwitz, but you certainly have researchers falling upon a dead child's skin!"

We become ultimate brothers through such based rapping, surviving by extracting the fatty lumps from diarrhea / skimming the bacteria off our fatty waste.

Imbalance ensues: Necrotypal patients chasing the basic, the single vapor of burning dollar-dragon.

What a disconcerting situation.

Predominant symptoms, unhealthy legal company; we end the study as reluctantly as it was started. The blade was only two meters away, but it did not matter; I took out my cock and yelled - "Join the club!"

it's not too long, but it does not mean that it's bad / it's not too bad, it's easy to use.

Their screams alert security.

He begins shrinking until barely visible, and finally says...

"Vagina."

and I, Vagina, banish some passable gak using his dirty works then excrete until diseased, like your mother, breastfeeding its cubs between contractions; her poetry, the diarrhea of a mangled heart.

Like some dump assed trolley in a river.

Or a markedly outdated Ausch joke?

You will say that separating was the correct thing to do for both of us, but it was truly for my personal enjoyment only; I am one of the world's greatest relationship experts, and have been tried and tested.

Neither confirm or deny my methods, and apply positive thinking to everything.

PARTAKE

BY AUSTIN JAMES

A MONTH before summer when cottonwood flakes float on nothing like paper ashes, the time of year when mother made her famous Caucasian Casserole with fried nipples and pancreatic sausage [doused in great-gamma's secret tonsil sauce]. Crockpot witchery. It's during this death rattle of springtime when I grind inside my husk, wearing corduroy flip-flops and drinking diet cocktails. Smoking fat-free cigarettes.

Backwards children frolic in the meadow below my nest, pointing, commenting on my laser white eyes. I crave slurping their slick ribs like sticky fingers.

Cracking open their knee joints to suckle upon like

freshwater mollusks.

Dipping their toes in Worcestershire and swallowing whole.

Even now the children throw rocks, hoping to knock me from my perch and watch me tumble, watch me smear into the ground. Watch me lick the gravel from my wounds. Scrutinize me whilst I piss on the tarmac clay, molding mud to pack against my ribcage swellings.

Fuck them and their youthful trickery. It's been so long since I chewed sinew, since I had the teeth for it.

Greedy tears overboil just from thinking it. The liver [or whatever organ resists within] sore and sour and altogether messy.

Hey there, a boy calls, *what are you doing, always dormant and wrapped within yourself up there?*

I'm never-neverlanding—I reply—would you like a taste?

Just a bit, I suppose, he says, climbing unto my roost. *Is it true what they say? The stories of your treachery?*

Kind of, depending on what you've heard and of which you are asking.

Lullabies of a flesh eater, a bone picker, the Wyvern Lord of the Anthropophagi. A monster that marinates children's hearts in liver juices.

Marrow, actually. Marinated in marrow, the slippery syrup of greater eras. Alas, I am no longer this eater of children, devourer of folk. I am old, and I decompose within my den, fatigued and starving [my voice: crackly and crooked].

Never again to indulge in human meat? The boy soaks upon the pain of this stanch old man.

Outwardly I laugh and sigh and giggle and cry. Inside I am young, just without the strength to pander in cannibalistic choreography.

Please, the boy says, offering a wrist, *drink from my bloodstream.*

Quiet, young one—I say—you know not of what you are asking.

Really, you must. I am alone in this world and will surely perish before long. Let me offer myself as sacrifice to the Erstwhile Gods so that I can die for a cause.

Snap of the neck, sip of the spinal juices, filling the cleft within my digestive tract. Tempt me once…

Tastes like fillet-o-fish, his dermis spattered within my guts, bloating my pores. Contemporary children are all poisoned by the mar of modern convenience. Their meat is tainted, near spoiled, only angering hunger aches. This putrid feed is why my kind are going extinct —not for the laws of man. They've chosen starvation. Except I, the stubborn old fool inside a cockleshell of denial and decay.

Under-tolling my words, I whisper to the boy's carcass: the Erstwhile Gods are all dead.

Vanished, you say? he asks as I gnaw at his bladder sac, my tarter-sauce-scent of stagnate and bowel-rot weakening in stench. *Understanding your prose is an uneasy task.*

Without a trace—I respond in blech—ergo, they must be dead.

Exterminated, maybe? the boy asks from within my veins.

You could be right—I ponder, the boy's skeleton scattered about the base of my perch. Younger children below play with his collar bone, toss his skull to and fro. Sword fight with his femurs, still wet with salivation.

Zero gods answer the cries of present generations—I proclaim, picking tendon scrapings from my teeth— that's the only thing left to comfort anyone, boy.

FOR A DRAGON'S KISS

BY J.L. MAYNE

THE GEARS CLICKED as James wound the watch; a tiny chittering, like a cricket singing its lonely song to the night. He pressed the crown and watched through cracked glass as the hands seemed to thank him as they slowly spun around the skeletal face of the clock.

Light streamed in as the windows shed their suits of black, revealing the bright sun reflecting from the glass-like ocean. The silhouette of the rotors created a halo above the helicopter's cockpit. James stared out the window at the expanse of water listening to the drone of the other passengers.

A tall man, Buck, sat across from James discussing the hunt with an Asian man, Long. Buck wasn't his real name, just what James thought his name should be. His voice was a southern drawl and he wore a fancy hat the color of cured wood. The gold buckle on the side of the hat looked like it was worth more than James had ever seen, or at least as much as his watch. Long's black suit looked cut from a slab of onyx by a god, the fine cloth perfectly accenting his sharp figure. He always dressed like that.

Long eyed James from across the cockpit, a tiger watching a biting fly buzz around its head.

"Like I was sayin'," Buck said, the words rolling out of his mouth musically, "a person of your caliber ought ta know that it'll be like any other hunt. Predators act like predators. Thing won't do anythin' to us if we don't provoke it."

"I believe this creature will not be like any other predator you have encountered. It was not made by natural selection; it does not have to follow any natural rules. It need only do what it is programmed to do." Long's accented voice was as sharp as his suit; as sharp as everything about the man. He gave James another half glance, inspiring James with a strong desire to dissolve into his seat.

"Nah, I still say it'll get some instincts from the critters they stole the genes from."

"Perhaps, but the technology to create such a creature is very precise. There is no evidence that the beast will act against its programming."

"I guess we'll see, Long."

"Yes, we shall see."

A pause in the conversation before Buck continued: "What does your name mean, anyway?"

A smile encroached on Long's stoic face. Humor maybe? "It means 'Dragon.'"

The humming voice of the helicopter's AI control unit instructed the passengers to fasten their seat belts. James Looked through the window at green trees only feet below. Brightly colored birds of red, yellow, and blue fled from the helicopter.

The helicopter slowed, leveled, and began to descend. The blanket of trees rose on all sides as they landed on the pad with barely a bump.

The doors on each side of the cabin opened with a hiss. A wave of scents rushed into the cabin. The sweet smell of ripe fruit seemed amplified by the humid air, and the thunderous roar of water drowned the sounds of the surrounding forest. James stepped out of the helicopter and turned to see a waterfall cascading down a towering cliff, the mist from the water crashing on the rocks, gently kissing his face.

The side of the helicopter was tattooed with the company's logo: "Lief Incorporated, the leader in all things technology." A decade earlier they had unveiled a virtual reality world. Then, only a few years later they outdid themselves with real-world experiences. One-way tickets for some consumers, all clearly labeled, not even in fine print. And you still had to spend a year on the waiting list.

A lithe figure stepped beside him. He turned to find Long's daughter, Miya. Her eyes closed and her head angled towards the sky. Her long dark hair flowed down her back, wisps of it fluttering and dancing with the shimmering mist. A silver chain around her slender neck glinted in the light.

James' heart fluttered and he felt like a ball of clay rest at the bottom of his stomach. His hand found its way to the crown of his watch and wound it methodically, the gears gratefully accepting the life his hand provided.

Miya never looked at him. She quietly stood in the twinkling mists as though bathing in gold.

———

James could swear he had seen the path before—a narrow ledge cut into the face of the cliff. One side stone, the other a death drop. Not uncommon were sections which had sloughed off, making it even more narrow. Stones ranging in size from pea to bigger than his skull littered the path where it had fallen from a higher section. He wondered how likely it was for one to fall from above, smash into his chest, knock him off the path and splatter his body across the canyon floor. Or simply kill him by pulverizing his brain.

Like ants, they climbed up the tiny trail. Legs moving in a steady march, the path slowly rising uncomfortably close to vertical. The switchbacks were not the typical rest with a wide area to turn. Instead, they were a ladder cut into the face of the gray stone. Wooden poles on each side acted as rails to aid in climbing. At the top of each ladder the path continued its slope up only to lead to another ladder, winding into the sky for what seemed like forever.

He looked up the cliff and considered why the helicopter hadn't simply dropped them off at the top. It was just another part of their adventure. An epic climb before a battle.

After his arms began to ache, James lost track of how many switchbacks they had ascended. The wood on each side—he thought it was bamboo—seemed to grow older with the rising elevation. More than once a sliver dug into his hands, the tiny pieces of wood searing his palms as though he had plunged them into fire. He started to wonder if he would be able to make it to the top of the next ladder. He stared at the pocked gray stone, dreading the climb as he placed his hand on the rail and looked up. This section had to be twice the length of the others.

Halfway up the ladder, his foot slipped on gravel. He frantically grasped at the rails as dust and rocks fell, hitting people below. Strings of curses and shouts of fear jumbled together from him and others.

For an instant, he was in the car, the world spinning as it flipped out of control.

He shook his head and continued up the ladder.

———

The breath caught in James' throat when he finally pulled himself to horizontal rock. Plateaus covered the entirety of the island, like teeth reaching up from the depths of the ocean and earth. Here and there, bright green trees, in their best effort to take hold on life, jutted out of the rock. A crystalline river ran from a distant peak, widening into a turquoise pool before tumbling from the cliff.

His gaze followed the rushing water. Moving a step away from the edge, he looked down into the chasm he had just crawled out of. The river was a thin line curling among rock and plants far below. He took another step back.

"Quite the climb eh?"

A voice battled with the wind and water to reach his ear, followed by a rough but friendly slap on the back.

James turned to see Buck smiling at him, a toothpick jutting from his mouth.

"Yeah, quite." James rubbed his biceps, remembering the ache they had developed.

"Arms hurtin'?"

"You could say that," James said, trying to act like they didn't hurt as badly as they did.

"Yep, me too." Buck flexed his right arm and rubbed a considerable bicep. "Thought it wouldn't, but I wasn't expectin' ta free-climb ten stories."

James nodded, his shaggy beard ruffling slightly from the wind.

"Gotta be honest, I wouldn't a put money on you makin it up here."

"Uh, thanks?"

"Nothin personal, you just don't look like someone who does much, uh, physical exertion."

Buck smiled and nodded to James' gut.

James returned the smile with a raised eyebrow and a frown. It wasn't a large gut, more like a pouch. James was proud of that pouch; he had been working out more than he could remember in almost his entire life. A girl could convince a man to do just about anything.

Buck took off his hat and scratched a bald head.

"Sorry," Buck said, "I'm not good with words. My ma always said I should think more before I spoke, rest her soul. What I'm tryin' ta say is, good job, and I look forward to workin' with ya."

He held out a calloused hand; James took it and they shook. He found himself smiling despite the insults from a moment before. He looked at his own hands, they burned and bled in places. He flexed them, trying to ease the pain and then began working at one of the splinters.

"Names Cooper, but you can call me Coop. Like a chicken coop. That's what ma friends call me anyway."

"James," James responded. "And you can call me James, that's what near everyone calls me. Except my mom, and you don't get to call me that."

"Call you what?"

"Nope, that's not even something you get to know."

"Fair enough," Cooper said with a laugh. "Wouldn't want her to hear it at any rate, would we?"

Cooper nodded over James' shoulder. James turned and found Miya rifling through some large metal boxes a few yards away. She wasn't hiding her frequent glances in his direction. Many of which were accompanied by a gorgeous smile. That smile, and those eyes. Even so far away James could get lost in those eyes.

James was pulled back to reality by another sharp slap on the back. "I'll leave you to it then mate, good luck with that one. She's a pretty one, but her father's a viper. Might have more luck courtin' that dragon."

James only half heard Cooper as he began walking towards Miya. He realized that the large metal box was a weapons crate. A katana was already strapped to her back, and she was now looking at bows. Others stood around similar crates selecting weapons of their own.

Glancing at James, Miya gave him a wide smile, holding it as she returned her attention to selecting a bow. The crate was wide enough to hold two, each on its own display.

James was suddenly aware of her father staring at them from another crate several feet away. He truly was like a viper, if a distracted one.

James wiped sweat from his forehead as it threatened to run into his eyes. He was sure it was from the heat, not the anxiety caused by the protective hound of a father, or the prospect of talking to an attractive woman. It was also at that instant that he realized he had moved. Curse his feet and their inability to remain a comfortable distance from anxiety.

"Ignore him." Her voice was like the coo of a dove at sunset.

Retrieving his ability to speak was almost as difficult as remembering to breathe.

"Uh."

"Very eloquent. I like a man who is good with words." Her Asian accent emphasized every syllable. She nudged him playfully and he knew he could die happy. "Which bow do you think I should choose? This one has a draw much too strong for me, but this one is only for shorter range. What do you think?"

The angelic woman held the bow for shorter range in her hand; the second still rested in the weapons crate on its rack.

James picked up the bow still in the box. The black coated steel gave a slight shine in the sunlight. He didn't know two bits about bows, but he was generally able to puzzle things out. That, and the overwhelming desire to impress the cute girl looking over his shoulder, removed any hesitation he had about the weapon. He decided to thank his feet later for succumbing to movement.

He just hoped the string wouldn't snap and cut out his eye.

It was a compound bow, the string winding up and back the length of the shaft. Where the sights should have been, there was nothing. He held the bow up as if to draw it and his index finger hit a button intended to be pressed naturally as you held the weapon. A screen came to life, projected in the air where the sights would have been. It enhanced an area directly in front of the bow with a cross-hair at the center.

"Damn, that's neat." He almost forgot that Miya was there watching him. Almost.

He held the bow up, not yet drawing it. The screen followed wherever he pointed the bow. 'NO TARGET' flashed on the reticle.

As James turned to put the bow away, it passed in front of the touch-pad at the front of the box. The screen of the touch-pad immediately lit up. An image of the bow filled the center of the screen with call-outs to various functions. The one that caught James' eye read "Automatic Strength Adjustment."

Miya was still looking intently. James tried to ignore her father as suggested as he wiped more sweat from his forehead.

"It looks like you can adjust the required strength for it." He handed it back to her. "Without looking at the others, this one seems pretty good."

She held the bow in her hand and pressed a small button on the inside of the bottom limb. James didn't notice everything that happened, but after a minute or so she was able to pull the string to full draw.

"Thank you. I don't think I would have noticed this otherwise. I think I will take this bow."

"Well, it was all... I mean, you're welcome." He held out his hand, regretting the gesture almost immediately and pulling it back. "I've missed you."

The words were out of his mouth before he could stop them.

"James."

It was then that Long intervened. A slew of angry sounding words in Chinese bellowed from the small man. James was sure most of it was for him, although he didn't understand any of it. Miya shouted back at him with an equal ferocity.

After an eternity or two of the battle between father and daughter, Long finally left in a rage, throwing a hand into the air wildly. James was glad the menacing halberd the man carried was for the dragon.

Miya clasped James' hand before hurrying to catch up to her father.

"Viper." Cooper was back at James' side. "Steer clear of that one." He idly flipped a stick in the air and caught it again.

"I really don't know if I can."

"Well, if ya have -"

"What the hell is that?" James stared open mouthed at a huge green gun Cooper had strapped to his back; a red Spartan helmet was etched into the side of the barrel.

"Ah, this? Don't rightly now. Some kinda laser gun, I think. Wanna hit the bastard hard. This'll do the trick."

James gawked for a few seconds before remembering that he still didn't have any weapons of his own. Cooper noticed.

"Better hurry," Cooper said, nodding toward the assembling crowd near them. "They probably won't wait long, and you wouldn't want ta' miss all the action."

A short time later, James was rushing to catch up to the departing crowd with a heavy pack slung across his back, a knife strapped to his hip, and a rifle in his hands. He almost felt like he was overdoing it, but they were planning on fighting a huge mythical beast. There probably wasn't such a thing as overdoing it.

Everyone carried packs of varying sizes, though his looked bigger than most. He needed one that would fit the large egg-shaped object he grabbed at the last minute. Despite the size of the bag, one end of the egg stuck out of the top. James readjusted his pack and hoped they didn't need to travel too far.

"You got any bandages in that purse o' yours?" Cooper asked with a chuckle. "My mum always had a few in hers, wasn't quite as big though."

"Ah, shut up," James said, though he appreciated the carefree banter and companionship.

"Here," Cooper said, handing James what looked like a silicone bracelet alongside earplugs.

"What's this?" James said, slipping the bracelet onto his wrist.

Cooper pulled his arm back with the large stick in hand. Stunned, James threw his arms in front of his face to protect himself from the attack. A crack in the air accompanied a blue glow which then blurred and vanished. A piece of the stick had broken and went zipping in a tangent direction, nearly hitting a man in the head.

Cooper held his stomach, almost collapsing from laughter. His toothpick fell from his mouth to the ground. "Your face! Man, was that worth it."

———

The entrance was big, like a huge meteor cut straight through the ground at an angle. Rocks of varying sizes, though all larger than a car, littered the area immediately around the hole. The sides of the rocks closest to the hole were charred black, frozen in smooth drips as though the hard stones were wax candles.

James walked up to the threshold and looked into its depths; a polished descent into darkness.

It was then that he realized it was silent. The drone

of voices which persisted through the climb and hike were now suffocated by the realization that this was real. They stood before the lair of a dragon.

"Fifteen."

It took a few long breaths for James to realize Cooper was standing next to him and a few more to realize he should respond.

"Wha?"

"Fifteen. That's how many we got here."

James looked around at the others standing to his left and right. Cooper's hat was in his hands. Another toothpick bobbed in his mouth as he spoke.

"You know how many they say you need?" Not a tinge of emotion surfaced in Cooper's voice. "Thirty."

James stared ahead. The scent of sulfur stung his nose.

"And," Cooper continued, turning and nodding his head towards some of the crowd, "I think they're fixin' ta leave."

James looked in the same direction as his companion. A group of five were walking away. Their weapons tossed into the opening like trash.

"Guess they don't have the balls for it," Cooper said, watching them go.

A breeze whistled past James' ears. Turning back with the others seemed like a sensible idea.

"Lot a money to spend on a short trip to a hole in the ground."

James nodded.

"Why'd ya come?" Cooper asked.

James hesitated. "I just wanted to see a Dragon. A real one. Not one of the glorified lap dogs with scales and wings. A real, fire-breathing, son of a bitching dragon."

"Yep, same as all of us, I guess. Amazing how much money people will spend just for an experience. Especially one that'll bite your face off."

"Yeah, just seemed worth it. You?"

"Me?" Cooper said, "Me too. Want another notch on my belt. That, and I want ta shoot this big green chiropractic bill on my back." Cooper shrugged and adjusted the large weapon at its mention. The huge gun looked like it weighed more than all of James' gear combined.

"Though," Cooper continued, "Doesn't seem to me like that's the only reason you're here. Better put those plugs in yer ears."

James felt his watch. Cooper was right. He looked at Miya. She was speaking with her father. If only he could have stayed. He wanted to. *She* had wanted him to. But Long would never allow it.

Exhaling, he stepped into the lair, Cooper beside him. It wasn't long after that he heard the sound of the other eight following them. He was surprised by the plugs as he slipped them into his ear canals. Sounds seemed amplified. He could hear every footfall, every breath from those around him. He had used similar before, but nothing this technologically advanced.

From somewhere deep within the earth, the dragon roared. Dust and rock hit James' head, knocked loose from the sound reverberating from the cavern walls.

As they walked, the sunlight dimmed, revealing purple, blue, and green fungus lining the furthest reaches of the tunnel. The rifts and fissures of the rock glowed as though luminescent blood leaked from unhealed wounds. Bright glow worms slid along the rock in search of scum and fungus. With the radiated natural light, there was no need for artificial.

Another, louder roar echoed through the long tunnel.

The lights from the worms winked out, leaving only the pale glow of the mushrooms to light their way.

Not fifty yards ahead of the group, James thought he could see glowing eyes in the dim light. A heartbeat later it was gone, leaving only blackness.

"I think I saw it," James whispered. His heart threatened to explode out of his chest. He thought he could hear Cooper's as well.

"Yeah." Cooper's voice came out in a squeak.

James doubted that the hours of classes and the scenarios he had run through in the simulator would be anything like what lay ahead.

James and Cooper led the pack further into the abyss. The quiet steps behind them resumed once the two found the will to move forward.

"Why doesn't it just fry us?" James whispered. His voice trembling.

"Wouldn't get many people out here if they all died in the first few seconds."

"Do you know anyone who's ever done this?"

The only response was the sound of shoes quietly caressing stone.

They reached the spot where the glowing eyes had been and a huge room opened before them. Thousands of lights dimly lit the walls as though they were inside an illuminated geode or drifting through the void of space. In the incandescent beauty, James forgot himself.

He imagined those lights were stars, and that beside him, he felt the warmth of a girl snuggled against his chest, her hand clasped in his as they watched for shooting stars, wishing that the moment would never end. Wishing that he and the girl weren't separated by worlds.

He thought of the accident, of blood running down

his face, Miya screaming as she was pulled from the car by men in demon masks. And he thought of Long.

James pushed the memories from his mind. He clasped and spun the crown of the watch, winding it as though it held the memories within its glass, winding it as though time would go back to that night under the stars, as if it would erase all the bad. He idly spun the bracelet on his wrist, doubting the piece of plastic would do much good against anything larger than a small rock. Or a stick.

They stopped a few paces inside the room of the cave. The others in the group lined up along both side walls. Clicks and hums sounded as they all readied their various weapons. The glow of holographic screens and reticles added to the dim light.

James clicked off the safety of his gun and felt his belt for the extra magazines. He also happily noticed Miya standing near him, nocking an arrow.

Near the cavern wall opposite the group, a large swathe of the lights blinked out. Two glowing purple eyes replaced them, hanging unblinking in the darkness.

"You see that too, right?" James' voice cracked despite the whisper.

"It is just watching us." Miya's voice barely cut through the air to James, even with the ear-plugs.

Gunshots erupted. Muzzle and laser flashes blinded. Sparks flew from the rocky walls of the caverns as bullets ricocheted. James darted to his right, trying to get a wall behind him, the flash of guns illuminated a huge clawed reptilian hand as it cut a man in two.

James stood in shocked horror at the carnage, not firing a single round. What good would his gun be? A man was thrown into the darkness by what looked like a spiked tail. Men and women ran in all directions, some to the opposite side of the cavern, others back the way they came. James stood as though a mannequin, dumb and unable to move. Unable to breathe.

Suddenly, blessedly, the maelstrom subsided. Screams of agony echoed through the darkness. Few of the fungi and worms gave any hint of illumination and flashlights slowly clicked to life. James remembered his light and clicked it on. He hadn't needed it before because of the glow of the flora. Now he chastised himself for not turning it on sooner.

With the light, his legs remembered how to walk. He made his way to the rest of the group, trying to piece together what had happened. The man he thought had been cut in two was standing, rubbing at his back. He now saw that only one person was seriously injured, and not directly by the dragon. A large rock had fallen from a wall and crushed the man's leg. Cooper and three other men were in the process of pushing it off. The man's shield sputtered, attempting to protect him from the boulder pinning him. Miya knelt beside the man, ready with bandages and hemostatic powder.

James felt the band on his wrist. Thinking back on the battle. It was like the dragon was toying with them. A cat with a mouse, watching them run in futility. He realized that at least some of the lights he had thought were lasers and gunshots must have been the shields taking the blunt of the attacks. Incredibly, no one was dead. The shields were much more durable than he'd thought.

The man with the crushed leg screamed as Miya bandaged him, but she stopped the bleeding. He would live. Miya attempted to calm him with caressing words while at the same time her father berated the two of them, Miya for helping him and him for being a fool and getting his leg crushed.

James closed his eyes and saw blood, men dragging Miya away from him as others kicked him in the stomach. Long with a stream of blood flowing over one eye, a gun in his hand.

"Hey, get over here." Cooper's voice cut through his stupor.

James hurried over to a small group.

"Needless ta say, we got our asses handed to us," Cooper said.

"Did you see that thing? It's a fucking cyborg," said James.

"Yep thought we were dead," a blonde woman said. Her hand rested atop a pistol on her hip and her shirt was cut low. James forced himself not to stare.

"We probably are dead," someone else said.

"Well, we need a plan." Cooper looked around at the group. A few others came to join as well, including the few which fled when things got messy.

The group argued about what went wrong and what they should do to remedy it. The truth was, everything had gone wrong, and having any plan at all would increase their chances of not getting fried.

———

It wasn't much of a plan, but anything had to be better than nothing. They weren't confident that the shields would be able to last more than a couple hits. At least their strategizing got everyone moving.

A handful of gun-light beams were the only thing separating them from complete darkness. After the last passage, not even the glow worms and fungus remained. James took note of the black rock as his light swept across the wall. It looked much like the mouth of the cave, charred and melted.

James moved with Cooper and Miya. Long trailed the group, as though ensuring no one could escape.

"I have missed you too," Miya's whispered voice sang to him.

"I-" James' stammered, trying to form words with a numb tongue, "I'm sorry. I should have stayed, should have-"

"No, you could not have." Her voice remained quiet but became stern. "My father never would have allowed it. I am surprised he did not load me back onto the plane the moment he saw you."

"Miya," James wound his watch, "why do you let him control your life?"

"He is my father."

"Yes, but- that night, there's nothing-"

"No, you do not understand." She took his arm. "I see you still have your watch."

James caressed it. "Are you kidding, I could never get rid of it."

"Even broken?"

"Our breaks make us what we are."

They finally came to a huge room. Stalactites and stalagmites framed the room like the inside of a dragon's gaping maw.

Simultaneously, their lights began to flicker. Muttered curses littered the air, and one by one the lights went out.

James stood in the dark and silence. The rapid drum-beat of his heart filled his ears, deafening in the muted air.

Ahead, a faint purple glow hung in the darkness. Radiant tendrils blossomed, brightened and expanded, following the curves and edges of muscle and machinery, outlining the huge shape of the dragon. Its wings were folded behind its back. Its eyes glowed like a royal fire. Hard scales abruptly met metal midway across its face. The entirety of the beast's body was an intertwined mass of sinew and wires, metal and bone. Lights danced across and through the wires like veins reaching out to the extremities before returning to the center, the heart, beating an ethereal glow of death and life. A cacophony of animal and technology bred into a beautiful abomination of nature.

The dragon sat, staring, considering. Its eyes blinked from time to time, blocking the violet glow for a brief instant. Thin tendrils of smoke licked the air from the dragon's nostrils, barely visible in the pale light. James wondered if it was deciding to eat him, or just burn him to a crisp.

He could hear the breathing of the others quicken in anticipation. Miya grasped his arm tighter.

He looked to his right and saw Cooper, the huge green gun trained on the beast ahead. Miya let go of his arm and stood, beautiful and ferocious. An arrow nocked in her bow, the metal head glinted in the dim light.

A shot rang out from behind the lead group; the flash casting brief, eerie shadows. Sparks flew from the metal of the dragon's face, lingering half a heartbeat in the darkness. The dragon's head barely moved, but its eyes billowed with rage.

The dragon's released an earth-shattering roar. A maelstrom of mechanical and feral animal fury pummeled the plugs in James' ears. Without them, he didn't doubt he would be deaf.

Massive arms and legs flexed and it leapt toward them. James jumped to the side, rolling out of the way just as the beast landed where he had been an instant before.

It didn't stop to consider him, but darted for the source of the gunshot; dust and rock flew into the air as its claws tore at the ground.

Idiots! James thought. This wasn't part of the plan. He raised his rifle and began firing.

He turned to see more gunfire. Blinding flashes from gun powder and lasers. In the flashes he could see Cooper taking aim with his massive green cannon. Just as the cannon fired, the dragon dodged. The red beam crashing into the wall, rocks exploded, narrowly missing the people below.

James found Miya on the opposite side of the room. She loosed an arrow which hit the dragon in the back and clattered to the floor. She shook her head and reached for another, pressing a few buttons on the quiver before removing it. She drew and fired, a lime trail of light followed the arrow through the cavern. An explosion of green liquid showered onto the dragon's side. It let out a pained scream before turning toward Miya, dropping a man it clutched in its clawed hand.

Miya's eyes widened as the huge creature charged her. She turned to run as James raised his gun and fired. The bullet struck the area wounded by Miya's arrow. A burst of scales and blood cascaded to the ground. The dragon lurched from the shot and lost balance, crashing headfirst into the wall, feet from where Miya now stood panting.

Gunfire continued to pelt the animal, still doing little damage. James could see the familiar red beam of light from Cooper's laser pointed at the ceiling above the dragon. Seconds later, the red-hot beam darted through the air and slammed into the hard stone. A huge chunk of rock broke, falling towards the dragon below.

Just as the dragon raised its head, the rock slammed into its back and neck. Wires sparked and blood ran down its back as the dragon swiped a huge rock, hurling it through the air straight at James.

Black, and then light. He was crawling out of the car, trying to reach Miya as she was drug away by the demons—red masks with black eyes. One of them pulled him out. James punched him in the face and stumbled to his feet. Another kicked him in the chest, knocking him to the ground.

He watched as Miya was pulled towards a black sedan. Long had warned them of this. Warned him that he had to protect her. He was too weak. He tried to stop it, but was helpless against the men. Blood ran from his mouth. Long stumbled from around a car.

James shook his head, trying to regain his thoughts, his vision spinning. It seemed the shield had worked again; and his luck.

He wiped his arm across his face and found a trickle of blood flowing from his mouth. Not bad considering what had just happened. He sat up, only to witness the dragon in its full fury.

Two men were thrown across the room, their bodies smacking like rag dolls against the cavern wall. The dragon rose on its back legs and roared as they slid life-lessly to the floor.

It then turned to two other men as they attacked, its mouth opening wide; James could see dust swirling in the air towards the dragon's mouth and into its lungs. Seconds later, purple flames burned through the air. James watched as the men's shields glowed blue in a feeble attempt to ward off the inferno. They held for mere seconds before failing and exposing the men, their arms raised as flesh melted from bones and bones disintegrated into ash.

James felt a light touch on his back and turned to find Miya looking at him with fear filled eyes as she set the backpack near him.

"Perhaps we can use this," she said, voice quivering.

James nodded and began pulling out the egg-shaped device as cooper crawled up to him on his other side.

"Well holy shit," Cooper said, "what's that thing?"

"A drone," James replied as he pressed a button on the egg's side. The egg unfolded and revealed four propellers which spun immediately, lifting the drone into the air and revealing a control module beneath. James picked it up and began guiding the drone toward the dragon. Cooper, to his left, adjusted the Laser cannon on his shoulder.

"I've only got one shot left. Better make it count."

Miya stood near James. Her bow lay in pieces on the ground. She held her sword in one hand. James doubted it would do much good, but he did think it was pretty hot having an attractive, badass girl near him wielding a sword.

Ahead of them, the survivors dodged flames and strikes. Long wielded his halberd, screaming at the monster. James doubted they could last much longer.

He pressed the button on his control screen, streams of laser fire shot out of the drone at the dragon's head. It turned to face the drone, shielding its face with one clawed hand and swatting with the other.

"Cooper, fire that thing!" James screamed as he launched a rocket. The small projectile shot out of the drone, a trail of white smoke behind it. The dragon wailed as it was hit in the shoulder, falling back and spewing purple flames wildly.

Cooper had already pulled the trigger and the gun powered up. A few infinitely long seconds later, the beam of red light fired, hitting the dragon in the stomach.

The beast roared and fell onto its back, kicking its legs violently into the air as bullets and lasers pelted its underside.

The dragon rolled, releasing a half circle of violent purple flame. No one was hurt, but it gave the dragon time to stand. It stared at Cooper, and charged.

James saw Miya running forward with her katana straight at the dragon. He followed it with his drone. It had a visible limp, but still covered the ground at an incredible pace. It paid no mind to Miya, reserving its rage for Cooper who was slumped against the wall in defeat, the green gun sitting uselessly at his side.

James thought of the car crash. Letting the emotion rush into him.

He thought of the men taking his bride to be. Of the tears mixing with his blood as the men beat him. Of how useless he had felt.

He saw Long, gun in hand. Mercilessly shooting the men in the back. Not a viper. A dragon, protecting his most precious treasure.

The men kicking him had run. Long killed them too. And let James lie in the street. Defeated. Not worthy of his daughter. How could he be worthy when he could not protect her?

James fired his remaining rockets. The charging monster shrugged them off as blood, scale, and metal were torn from its body. The rounds for the drone's laser flashed red. He pressed a button and 'SELF DESTRUCT' began flashing on the screen. He slammed the directional controls forward and the drone raced towards the dragon.

The ferocious demon loomed over Cooper, and in turn James. He knew they were going to die. He tried to ignore the huge looming shadow and focused on the screen in his hands. He ran the drone into the dragon's back. At the same instant, he pressed the self-destruct button.

A huge explosion ripped open the air and pushed the metal monster to the ground, its jaws narrowly missing Cooper. Sparks flew as bits of ichor pelted James.

With the beast incapacitated, Miya slammed her katana into the dragon's side between scales, burying the blade into flesh. She pressed a button on the sword's hilt and an explosion tore open the dragon from the inside. More metal and sinew rained down around them.

The dragon released a pained groan and tried lifting its head. Sparks and smoke accompanied blood as the whine of dying bone and gears ground together. Its eyes closed, and it went limp.

Cooper stumbled up to James, covered in saliva and salt from the dragon's breath. He wiped his face and shook his head. James could see now that one of Cooper's arms was missing. He hadn't noticed the dragon's flames, but could see that the wound was cauterized. He was sure Cooper would have died otherwise.

"Let's get the hell out of here," were the only words spoken as the three walked out of the cave.

———

James stepped out of the cave and into the sunset, his hand clasped in Miya's. Long bowed his head to the two of them.

Cooper wasn't far behind them, insisting that he was well enough to walk himself out and talking about what bionic arm he could get to replace his old one.

James stared at his reflection in Miya's eyes. He could get lost in those eyes. Countless times he had been lost in those eyes.

"You kept your promise." Miya stared back at James, her smooth lips always in a smile for him. "You told me that you would prove it to him."

"I didn't know if he would come."

"He has always trusted his daughter."

She pulled the necklace from her shirt. A curled gold and silver Chinese dragon clung to the chain. Two ruby eyes glinted back at them. Next to the dragon, a golden ring.

She took his hand, running her fingers along his palm to the crown of his watch. She wound it, the tiny clicks taking in the life she offered.

She kissed him, and he knew that he was hers.

WHAT'S IN YOUR HEAD

BY DONALD ARMFIELD

And the blue giant of Spica
went kicking around in the
      night sky.
Following the arc from Arcturus,
over the celestial equator
then the luster of Virgo
dances in the skies.

The feast with our Lady of
      Sorrows,
will be exquisite,
let us dine in cheer.

And the seven daggers' rueful
      display
will hopefully not bleed this time.
The star has been born and the
      head,
will begin to cluster its memories.

And yet, the whispers still argue
with the faithful departed
Help us bury this hatchet
where the roses will grow again.

Her ancient Gregorian chants,
Cheerless or tragic melancholic-
      hymns
that drape over organ basslines
      and
stain the fingertips of catgut
      strum.
And all who sing along helps call
her beast to come forth.

A winged creature so large and
      powerful,
intelligent and beautifully scaled,
the color of ash.
The fire she spits turns the evil to
      stone,
and its attackers to soot.

The dragon rider she is, our lady,
the lovely Irish singer is the
      only one
to tame such a beast.

2

The feast as expected
but jealousy turned the tables
and the serpent was frowned
    upon.
The men swung with useless
    power,
like trying to pierce a rock,
with the stem of a rose.

The town burned to the ground,
and what remained was too little,
too little to build upon.

And so she stood in the center
of it all, patting her winged beast,
looking over at another fallen
    town.

Why must they try, or are they
    afraid?
You are my gorgeous creature,
oh how I love thee, if all that
    remains
is ash at our feet...
let them know there is a picture.

A picture in my head of
cheers after the feast under a
    night sky,
no arguing whispers amongst the
    jealously

a buried hatchet and acceptance
   of this beast.
My dragon, my beauty, you lovely
   creature.
Why must they hate?

DANCING WITH FIRE

BY DR. BENJAMIN ANTHONY

---

gotta keep the devil way down in the hole

— TOM WAITS

My sneakers were grazing the sidewalk; was still floating, but almost back on solid ground. The last lines of dragon bone I had snorted were wearing off. My body was losing the magic it had briefly gained, so it was time to find my dealer, Smog.

Smog was a big dude. He must weigh four hundred pounds, if not five hundred. He kept a bright green mohawk on his head and his arms were a mass of indistinguishable tattoos of skeletons and dragons and naked ladies. His earlobes were stretched out to hold rubies the size of silver dollars and his nose was a ladder of silver rings that went from the nostrils up to his eyebrows. He dealt powdered dragon bone to whoever could afford it and knew the right words.

The first time I tried snorting powdered dragon bones I breathed fire and flew across the city skyline. I was unstoppable. The rooftops and streetlights were far below me; I spit balls of fire into the air and couldn't believe how strong I felt. When I eventually came down, I slowly drifted back down to the ground, coughing little clouds of smoke every time I tried to go higher. I snorted the rest of the bag that night.

Couldn't wait to get my hands on more and I've been getting more and more the past three years. In that time I have found some of the side effects of snorting powdered dragon bone include taking on the characteristics of a dragon, mainly scaly skin and fire breath that comes out when you cough or sneeze. Wisps of smoke constantly drool from my nose, mouth and, when I'm extremely agitated, even my ears.

Smog hung out around a park a few blocks from the water's edge, surrounded by little cafes and pizza places and the local courthouse. Drug dealers are nothing if they aren't bold. Dealing dragon bones right in front of the same people who would lock them up for ten to twenty years takes a certain kind of fearless game that not every player has.

Smog was filled with an icy game, along with fat stacks of cash to pay off numerous rats in the police force. I found him lounging on a bench, talking on his phone in a foreign language while a half a dozen of his crew moped around. A radio was on the sidewalk blasting some incoherent European rapper. All I could make out was something about pussy and money and weed in between heavily accented mumbling. What's with this shit kids listen to now? I made my way over to Smog, who acknowledged me with a slight nod.

"I'm looking for the king under the mountain." I tried to say as quietly as I could and held out a fist bump with a couple of wadded up fifties inside it.

Smog looked at my fist like it was a roast beef sand-wich and licked his lips. One of his crew, a girl in shredded jeans and a bikini top that showed off her alli-gator-like skin, hard edges, bumps and scales, fist bumped me and grabbed the wadded cash. She flashed a quick smile and pointed one finger up in the air, the sign that a hundred dollars worth of dragon bone was mine. Smog nodded at me again and continued talking on his phone.

I looked around, unsure who had my bag of dragon bone. Where was it? The crew were still moping around, the music blared on, sunset was still a few hours away, nothing had changed, except my pockets growing a hundred dollars lighter.

Then I heard a whistle.

Two short shrill sounds that came from one of the trees about twenty feet away. I walked over and heard a voice from the branches above me.

"Yo! Catch this shit."

A little bag fell through the air; my reflexes were quick and I caught it before it hit the ground. I stuffed it in my pocket and glanced up into the tree, but nobody was there. I took a quick peek at the baggie. It was wrapped in a piece of paper with some writing on it. The bag looked to be the right size so I jammed it back in my pocket and flattened out the paper to see what it said.

500 keys - Wisconsin - 11pm dockside

I looked around again, Smog and his crew were still in the same spot, music blaring away. The paper had to be a note for someone other than me, but I didn't dare give it back.

When I first tried dragon bone, I thought it'd be like any other drug. Done my share of coke and pills and even tried junk for awhile, but all those highs weren't real. They all ended and only left me wanting something more. They didn't really change me, just left me feeling used. Dragon bones gave me something real, though. Dragon bones let me fly, really fly, not just hallucinations and I could breathe fire.

Breathing fire is not to be taken lightly. After my first few bags of dragon bone, I burnt down my apartment complex. It wasn't a big place, only four units, one of those old double wide houses with the upstairs and downstairs divided into shitty apartments on both sides. The fire marshal couldn't figure out exactly what caused the fire, though he suspected someone was cooking meth, but there weren't the tell-tale toxic chemicals lingering around to prove him right. After that I took to living in my van and crashing at friend's houses.

The high was so complete, it was almost unreal. The changes it made to you were permanent, horns and spikes growing out of your body, skin turning into hard scales and nails turning deadly sharp. This wasn't some cheap drug junkies and hippies were still ending their lives with. This was something worth basing your life around. I was turning into a dragon!

Pico, my girlfriend, snorted a line of powdered dragon's bone and shuddered as she floated from the couch and into the smoke-filled room. Her eyes grew large and danced with fire as she stared at me.

"You look more and more like a dragon every time we do this shit!" She giggled as saliva dripped off her tongue and hung from her mouth.

My line of powdered dragon bone was a bit fatter than Pico's as I had been a user longer than she had. I floated into the air and coughed a cloud of smoke.

"Maybe look in the mirror sometime, babe; you got horns coming out of your eyebrows and your skin feels like a snake's asshole!" I rubbed up against Pico in mid-air, letting her long forked tongue glide over my face as I joked with her.

Only it wasn't a joke. Pico really looked more and more like a dragon every day, even when we were out of the powder she still seemed to be changing, transforming, evolving, turning into something else. We would be dragon lovers in a little while. It would be hard to go out in public, but when you can fly and breathe fire it doesn't matter.

I looked at the paper I got with the bag, it had to mean that a deal was going down on the docks tonight, a big shipment, five hundred kilos of powdered dragon bones were going to be coming in on a ship named the Wisconsin. That would be enough powder to turn me and Pico into full blown dragons, we'd never stop flying.

Anyone who got in our way would be burnt to a crisp with one sneeze.

We were curling through the sky and I had to tell her I was gonna get that powder. A plan was forming in my brain, and the more I thought about it, the more I knew it would work.

"Look babe, we gotta try this. We can swoop in there and grab all that powder and be gone before anyone knows what's going on, then we'll be set for years with that much weight. We'll be real ass dragons and we'll be able to do anything we want! Never touch the ground again cause we're so high! C'mon with me babe?"

Pico looked doubtful.

"But they're gonna have guns and shit, no way they'd move that much powder and not have some heavy dudes around to guard it!"

I arched away from her in the sky, pulled my shirt up and grabbed the pistol tucked into my pants. She gasped, not knowing what I was doing. I pointed it back at myself and let off a round.

The bullet stuck in my skin, but didn't get through my tough dragon hide. I pulled the bullet from my chest where I had shot myself and held it up for her to see.

"Okay." Was all she had to say.

I rented a moving truck to transport the haul and drove down to the docks. Since she didn't even look human anymore, Pico stayed in the back.

The smell of fish and gasoline greeted me as I drove around looking for the freighter. The docks had an industrial port and several small marinas and slips for recreational boaters. All the public docks allowed me to get a good look at where the Wisconsin was tied up. It looked like an ore boat, but I had no idea how the powdered dragon bone would be stored, or who would be moving it off the boat. The security gate was still staffed, so I parked the truck a couple blocks away in front of a breakfast diner that was closed for the night.

My plan was to snort a little more powder so I would be flying high, then sweep down on the Wisconsin and grab the shipment when I saw it. I knew that whoever was unloading it would be armed, but I had skin that bullets wouldn't be poking any holes in and I'd be breathing fire on their asses. I got out of the truck and went to the back to let Pico out as I coughed up a small cloud of smoke.

The door on the back of the truck rolled up and Pico was standing there, more dragon than when she had gotten in! Her arm stretched out and a single claw slid into my neck. Without any effort, she lifted me from the ground. She had done something to me; I couldn't move, couldn't struggle, and my neck felt funny. She started to giggle.

"Poor little boy. Not what you were expecting? Thought I was just some bonehead like you?"

I tried to gurgle out an answer, but only bubbles of blood formed on my lips.

"I forgot, you little boys can't even talk when I separate your vertebrae. I suppose I do owe you a bit of explanation, don't I?"

Smoke was pouring from Pico's nostrils, she giggled a little bit more and a jet of fire spewed out of her mouth, singeing the hair on my head.

"I forgot, you can't answer me. Well, you see, there was only ever one dragon, the rest of us are his bastard children. Like you, they took parts of him, ate his flesh, drank his blood and were transformed, grew into things that weren't quite dragon but weren't human either. The longer this went on, the weaker the bastards became, because they weren't from that original serpent, the only real dragon, but they were bastard children of bastard children. Copies of copies of copies, y'know? This whole time you never have snorted a real powdered dragon bone, just the parts from someone else who was using the parts from someone before them and on and on."

My mind was doing somersaults. I had found Pico one day after scoring a bag from Smog, and always thought she was just a kid who didn't know anything. But all this time, she was something else. What was going on? Why couldn't I move? Was I paralyzed or what?

"Now it's your turn, you can't go on like this, there's horns growing out of your back and your head for god's sake! You've been careful not to let people see your growths, but we can't expect you to keep them hidden forever. Now you get to be the powdered dragon bones some other shithead is gonna snort!"

Bubbles of blood kept forming on my lips and I wanted to scream but nothing came out. My whole body felt cold and wet. Things were getting dark but I could still see Pico's eyes dancing with fire as she threw me into the back of the truck.

THE LAST HUMAN

BY DANI BROWN

PLASTIC SKIN HADN'T BEEN BUILT to expand. Cracks gave way to fissures and released the flies, their wings scorched. They didn't get far. The opening became larger, spilling out a host of circuits and shiny bits of metal, melted around the edges. The skin bubbled as Gary pumped into her.

Cold eyes stared at him. They stopped blinking five minutes before, the programming lost beneath whatever was happening under her skin. A bit of plastic, not fully melted, stabbed his stomach. The heat below him combined with the need to pump into her as the circuits to control her motion were lost. Her stomach area gave off steam to condense on his fat.

The last person alive, he searched the Earth for a real woman to mate with. No one laid buried but rested on top of their twitching robots. He pulled bloated bodies away always to be greeted by the same empty hole in the abdomen where circuitry should have been.

The egg shells scattered around the planet made his skin crawl. Even in the middle of the desert, long after the power switched off and the sands had taken over, they were moist with white fluid. No matter where he travelled, it never changed. The dead flies had the same scorched wings, spread out from the robots and egg shells.

He pumped. The flies crawling around, not quite gripped by death, watched his arse rise and fall, grey hairs with the odd dark one stuck up from the crack.

The white fluid could have grown a mate, but he wouldn't survive to her maturity. Gary needed relief somewhere. His hand and a sock wouldn't do without anyone left alive to watch. He pumped, feeling the twinge in his balls.

He caught sight of large golden eyes every now and again, but they never came out to watch. He couldn't make it work without someone there. He tried to set up a sex bot without a giant hole in her abdomen on the other end of Facetime without any luck. He knew cold indifference circulated within her. If she had once been programmed for warmth, it didn't show, even from the other end of a phone powered by the sun.

His balls filled to bursting, as they were now, but he couldn't release all over his sheets. Not without a real woman to watch. It didn't matter how close he was, he just couldn't do it.

He pumped into the sexbot. Her eyes were blue. They weren't meant to look painted on, but they did. They didn't when he first slid in. He wanted a kiss, but only a real woman from his dreams could provide one.

He sped up, not noticing the dark shadow that passed over the doorway and lingered. Her abdomen cracked beneath him. Shards of plastic lodged in his flesh. His heart rate kicked up a few gears.

He closed his eyes. After all these years, he was ready to blow his load. He could only hope he wouldn't be shooting dust.

The air grew chilly. He couldn't see the room turn darker, but he felt it on his skin. It was too late. He had to keep going, otherwise he'd explode.

His balls contracted, hitting the plastic as the roof caught fire. The heat could be mistaken for his own, but not hers. A noise he hasn't heard in a long time escaped his throat and through his lips just as his balls released. There should have been an echo.

Heat didn't rise from him, or from the robot spasming below him. Room temperature climbed higher than body temperature until his hair hung limp with sweat. He didn't know why he bothered to wax it up. There wasn't anyone around to impress.

His balls convulsed. The robot convulsed under him, swallowing his seed and boiling it. A blister burst on the tip of his cock. Fluid rushed past it and onto the broken skin. But he couldn't stem the flow of ejaculation, regardless of how much it hurt.

The heat dried his eyes and even caused his sweat to evaporate into the air as soon as it formed. Part of the ceiling caved in. Embers rained upon the room. His crack hair caught. His balls convulsed. The robot swallowed his seed, sucking it away from his cock and past the lose flaps of skin that were once a blister. Plastic melted into his body.

Teeth bit into Gary's legs and pulled him away, his cock still releasing fluid past the flaps of the blister. Energy drained out of him with his ejaculate. He didn't have the will to turn around and see what had him.

The robots could have gone mad, but most of them lie dead or spasming beneath the bloated corpses of the rest of humanity. Gary pictured one with steam shooting up from its headless body as the fluid gave way to dust.

Mechanical wings fanned his face. His skin sagged, mingling with his beard. Dirt and cum built up in his balls over decades existed within the winkles.

He risked opening his eyes. Something sparkled in the distance. Wherever he was, it wasn't home. His body felt spent. His balls no longer hung to his knees. That didn't stop the blood pounding him into an erection.

His wrists cracked. Years of trying to relieve himself made it known each morning with dawn's early light. There wasn't a window to work out what time it was, or day. For the last human left alive, it shouldn't matter, but it did.

Gary's wrists pushed him up. His belly had pieces of plastic embedded in it. Her unblinking blue eyes stared into him and through him as if he weren't really there, using her for one purpose. The purpose for which she had been built. Cold, indifferent eyes.

He searched the world for a woman. For a man. For anywhere to plant his seed, ever since Andy died.

Egg shells littered the floor, their creamy white insides never dry. They wouldn't be. The air contained a humidity he didn't stumble across through his desert wanderings to ensure wetness. The desert sun rising over the broken shells should have turned the white filling to dust long ago.

He stood up, his feet unfamiliar with the splattering of stray jizz. A squawk echoed at him. The mechanical wings sang and fanned. His swollen fingers grabbed, missing when they took off in a flight of broken white feathers, revealing their wiring. They flapped, just out of reach.

Dizziness washed over him, all blood in his cock. The wall took his weight, the plaster crumbling away to rock, not boards and pieces of wood with hairs lost in them. Someone took the time to paint it bright pink, way back when the world housed an abundance of people.

The bloated population had time. Too much time on their hands to tinker with things that shouldn't be messed with. The DNA planted in the sexbot on a time lapse. Waiting. Love was nothing more than a myth. A status symbol to parade for curtain twitchers and basement dwellers.

The basement dwellers had the last laugh. But they were all dead now. Their corpses not buried. Gravediggers in short supply. No one bothered to programme the robots to perform simple disposal applications.

Too much manga. Too much jerk-off fantasy porn on prime-time television in the disguise of an epic series. A basement dweller's fantasy made by more successful basement dwellers.

Basement dwellers. And time. Too much time.

Everyone swiped left, no matter their sexuality. Gary pieced it all together from his wanderings searching for a mate. Scratchings on broken primitive electronics covered in a dig site worth of ancient spunk to be chipped away and snorted for the memories.

Crusty socks breeding their own ecosystems in

forgotten closets never gave birth to a baby. A monkey wouldn't do. DNA incompatible. The base parts fitted together better than historic Lego, with a lot less pain and tears. It didn't produce a human baby.

Primates became less. They had a hard-on for the sexbots too. And mutant babies to care for. By-products of Gary's experimental mating.

Feathers floated down, catching in his hair for the birdbrain look. Basement dwellers of the past died with feathers from their pillows embedded in their heads as they succumb to complications pumping into hungry sexbots.

Gary didn't want to die with the sexbot's plastic embedded in his belly flab. It shouldn't be so flabby. He came across a store of well-preserved ancient food loaded in sugar beyond the bleached bones of early dragons. Ancient tasted so good. Not so good for his teeth.

Basement dwellers wanted miniature dragons perched on their shoulders in all their profile pictures. Photo manipulation software never occurred to them. Even a filter and the right angle might have scored them a date and saved humanity for some other fate.

The bones became larger the further Gary travelled away from crumbling and scorched cities of the past, each step without relief, without someone to watch him blow his load, brought his balls lower.

The last person watched as he jizzed all over his sheets. Wings didn't decompose. Gary never found it odd that human and primate bodies were a gooey mess while dragons broke down to bone and leather wings.

No underpants could house his balls. No support system for something so bloated ever existed. The basement dwellers, the great inventors, bringing damnation, could get themselves off. Years of practice and they were masturbation experts.

Gary kept his beard and greying hair for years in top condition and the same style to jerk off while his reflection stared back. It never worked. Even the odd glimpse of a dragon's pupil failed to bring him a thrill.

The dragons left him to his wanderings once Andy died. Gary gave his body to them, spreading it naked on a table in the English summer rain. When Gary returned from his wanderings, the dragons rejected his offering.

The winter sun shone filtered through wings. A filter might have saved the world. A girlfriend to consume time spent tinkering around with biology. A species never existed planted within the programming of favourite sexbots.

Some of the basement dwellers were women, equally as guilty of tinkering with the way things were. Dead on top of twitching bionic penises, cold robotic eyes stared at them with indifference as their bodies took eternity to break down into a gooey mess not even the flies wanted to touch.

The flies wanted to lay their eggs inside the robotic cavities. Maggots incubated the developing dragons, keeping them warm as robots rested unloved in factories and warehouses, never knowing the feel of projectile ejaculation.

A simple filter and hiding certain entitled and unstable personality traits in chats until the person at the other end of the swipe or super-like agreed to meet. Personalities can change. Love changes everything. Entitlement doesn't love, neither does borderline. It hides in wait. Condoms break. Humanity is saved through sex. Both in terms of distraction and reproduction.

The dragons weren't mechanical. Their corpses

would lie twitching beneath the sun, like the discarded sexbots littering the planet. Littering the floor. Robotic arms twitched, unattached to anything. Toes. Fingers. The only bones were wires and mechanical penises.

Bleached bones of winged reptiles littered the deserts and the forest undergrowth. A robot graveyard covered in neon pink dust. No archaeological evidence of dragons existed until the first sexbots appeared on the consumer market. The prices dropped before the basement dwellers sacrificed their manga money for a glorified masturbation aide.

Their mothers kept them supplied with perfectly good socks purchased in bulk from the cash and carry with a business account. Looking after a basement dweller was a fulltime job. Population overload. They didn't die when their mothers conked out. There were services for ass-wiping and laundry and feeding and cleaning.

Genetic modification was a lucrative business. A little splice of DNA here and a little there, injected into chicken eggs held in the abdominal cavities of sexbots and incubated by maggots.

Everyone wanted their own pet dragon for profile pictures. A lot of money to be made, to be spent on services to replace mommy-dear when the technology to keep her alive went to breeding more dragons and producing sexbots with blinking eyes and added sophistication.

They were basement dwellers, where they lacked hygiene and general social skills, they made up for it in desire to charm non-sentient beings, programme to agree with every whim. The hatchling dragons ate maggots. Each generation grew larger until shoulders could no longer carry the weight and massive selfie-sticks were needed to snap a picture with both the dragon and basement dweller within the frame.

Dragons couldn't live in basements. They required wide-open skies to fly with the jumbo jets and wave at the passing rockets on their way to Mars. When they grew too big, the basement dwellers were left with only their sexbots and paid servers to bring them tubs of premium ice cream.

The money dried up as people copulated with robots. Each robot contained an egg with a baby dragon sleeping inside.

The wall gave way. The cavern went on forever. A robot graveyard for as far as the eye could see. He turned around. The exit must be somewhere else. Cold blank eyes watched him go.

Lost in a maze, he thought he went the way he came. His cock throbbed, crying for relief. Begging to go back and piece together a robot for use. Only check her cavities for eggs and flies. He couldn't go back. The walls changed to green without any clue to his location.

Light shone in the distance, down the tunnel. He walked through deserts, growing fat on stores of ancient food. There was always food, without anyone around to eat it. His stomach rumbled. He sniffed the air. Nothing. No faint hint of sugar.

Basement dwellers loved their sugary treats. When the dragons learned to exhale fire, they gave them instructions to burn down everything that didn't add sugar, wheat or corn to their diets. Samples of their own semen would have tasted better if they ate a pineapple every now and again, but they had sexbots to drink it. Each bot came with more features and less resistance and those big manga eyes that got them so hard.

Gary grew hot walking along the green wall. Something bothered to put his tattered old pleather jacket over a random printed tee-shirt so carefully selected from a cache he found, in case he found someone, even a visiting alien, to impress enough to mate with him. All humans ever did, everything they ever did, was to impress a potential life partner, or three, if one wasn't enough. Until sexbots.

Then they genetically engineered dragons because away from fetish social networking, dick pics weren't acceptable profile pictures. The dragons weren't to impress a potential mate, but to intimidate other basement dwellers. No mates existed for the basement dwellers of the past. Not unless they learned about how filters and a good angle can impress someone enough to date them.

His balls rubbed against his jeans. The last few grey pubes existed only because fabric didn't touch them. He walked closer to the glitter. His stomach rumbled. Desire for chocolate and not gold. He couldn't eat gold. The air grew hotter. He pushed his hair back, just in case a passing spaceship took pity on him, he wanted something to impress one with breasts and a nice rear-end. The same style provided a friend. The second to last human.

The planet wasn't dead, or even dying, but thriving since the species wiped themselves out, taking most of the primates with them. The fires started by dragons provided fertile soil for new life to spout up from the ashes. Plants didn't push out humans though. Only other humans did that.

He paused to take off his jacket. The thing had been with him for so long, he couldn't give it up, not even to hop onto a passing space ship and find something in the universe to carry his seed. He walked on. No aliens

would find him inside what he thought was a cave, plastered over and painted in bright colours.

No escaped existed within the robot graveyard. He
didn't think he would find it again, much to the annoy-
ance of his throbbing cock and heavy balls. He walked
until he was blind. Then, he walked some more, hand
trailing along the wall so he wouldn't lose his way. With
all the walking, he might burn off all the calories from
the ancient food he developed a taste for.

He crashed into a pile of solid metal. It felt hot
enough against his skin to melt and made a clattering
sound.

"Come closer."

"Who," he cleared his throat. It had been nine long
years since Andy died. Nine long years since he used his
voice. He was surprised it still worked. "Said that?"

"The last human and the first dragon. Together at
last. I am sick Mister Gary, as are you."

Self-consciousness washed through him. He knew the
ancient food sat heavy on his gut and gave him extra
weight to carry around. He didn't realise how much.

"What do you want from me?"

"Just you. Your seed."

"Take it."

Something lifted him up. He felt himself levitating,
but nothing apart from heat pressing down on him. He
chanced opening his eyes, they hadn't melted away after
all. Suction attached itself to his cock.

"You need the face of a pretty girl to watch, look
around."

The room lit up with thousands of screens, each one
contained the face of a woman, a different woman but
each one contained the favourite features of his dream
lovers.

"They're long dead, decaying on top of fake penises. Their pretty faces melted into goo. Their curves long run into the floorboards and mattresses and sofa cushions. They wink and move and cringe. Each one sent a video of a man jerking off over her pictures. None had any interest in seeing his cumshot or even knowing he wanked over her. They wanted to know the man behind the glittering career and penis. Sexbots weren't the only factor in killing humanity."

His balls shrunk as he floated in mid-air. They didn't convulse as they did before. With each swimming sperm, his mind dimmed until it was black. A nightmare and nothing more.

He woke in his own magnolia painted bedroom between his cream coloured sheets, penis rock hard. He switched on the lamp. The walls weren't plain, as they should have been. Sketches and paintings of dragons covered the walls. The TV at the end of the bed switched on. A giant pupil winked on the screen.

"A reminder Mister Gary. You've been given a second chance. A chance to find the perfect partner."

The TV switched off. His cock didn't seem as erect as it did before. A mass of sticky goo glued the sheet to his body. He peeled it away, revealing the creamy white fluid caught in his pubes.

His bladder cried out for his attention. Five more minutes in bed. He caught sight of his phone. Only four in the morning. Two minutes to relieve himself and forget the nightmare. He could sleep until noon. He needed the rest. He worked hard, chasing his dreams.

Dragon wallpaper appeared while he slept, plastered over the magnolia walls. He didn't realise such a thing existed.

He stumbled into the bathroom and pulled on the

light. Glass dragons lined shelves that weren't there when he stumbled in a few hours ago after too many months spent on the road. Urine hit the water in the toilet.

"Remember Gary. A second chance in an alternate reality. Sexbots are only now hitting the market. Don't let what happened in your world happen in this one."

He caught the mirror while he contemplated washing his hands and combing spunk out of his pubes. The cold water would bring him too far into the waking world to find sleep again. A dragon's pupil winked at him. An image of a woman flashed before him. His future wife. Not a bot. He walked out of the door backward, engraving her image in his mind.

Someone compatible. Someone to love and love him in return, with respect, not hatred and competition.

"Don't try to impress her. Show her who you are."

He fell into bed. The dragons were still there when he woke up to flies buzzing. The buzz of death. The blinds let in slats of light. The shadows on the dragons on the wall revealed piles. He squinted his eyes and looked, reaching for his glasses.

Egg shells covered in creamy white liquid stared back, between the piles of twitching flies.

THE WIND ROLLER
BY MAXWELL BAUMAN

"The wayward wind, is a restless wind."

— GOGI GRANT

IT WAS MARCH 1996, and we were filming an episode of "Supernatural Searchers." It was going to be a paranormal investigative program for TLC. We had already taped a few shows, and for this episode we were tasked with finding evidence of the Wind Roller, a dragon spoken of by the Paiute tribe, rumored to have created the wind itself. Matthew Salak, Cameron Fisher, and I ascended Oregon's Steens Mountain. Salak was our cameraman, Fisher handled the sound, and I was the face, stage name Mystery Mike, here to uncover the unknown.

It was windy and overcast. Perfect weather for the kind of footage we were after. Salak pointed out we should get a shot of the wind blowing my hat away. Great for a laugh. He was always looking for the perfect shot, and was willing to push himself just a little farther to get it, even if that meant hanging off a cliff. Fisher, balancing a fuzzy boom mic and recording bag, scowled because the wind kept washing out my voice, but he always made it work.

We reached the summit, but to no surprise, didn't find the Wind Roller. There wasn't much to go on based on the legend, just that they created the wind and lived somewhere on Steens Mountain. At the time, I thought it would kind of look like Puff the Magic Dragon. Something green and silly like that. Or maybe it would be something classier, like a dragon in the corner of a medieval map blowing a gust of wind. But these things happen in show business, and with the right editing it would get on the air no problem. We called it a wrap on the shoot.

On our descent, we made our way down to the Alvord Desert at the base of the mountain. I was half day dreaming about a dragon blowing a current over the desert, playing with the shape of the dunes below. It was Salak who had turned back around to get another shot of the peak when he spotted an opening in the mountain we hadn't noticed when we began our climb. The mouth of the cave was long and narrow and covered by a loose overhang of grass. It would've been easy enough to miss if it wasn't for Salak's sharp eye.

I pulled the grass curtain aside. I expected to find beer cans and other trash left behind by teenagers, but there were better odds of stumbling across a wolf pack or bear protecting her cubs. It was always important to keep in mind when hunting for monsters like Big Foot or the Loch Ness Monster that the real danger could come from miscalculating the terrain or encountering wild animals. When nothing jumped out at us, I waved my crew to follow me. There was a low ceiling and we had to crouch to go inside. Large basalt stalagmites were packed in tight across the ground. They were formed by the lava that dripped down from thin, deformed stalactites overhead 15 million years ago. We had to leave most of our gear by the entrance to navigate. It wasn't easy to move at first, but more room started to open up the further in we went.

Past the light of the opening and stalagmites were several large cylindrical clay carvings standing upright with deep grooves spiraling around them. Each was about ten feet tall. There were more of these cylinders of varying sizes deeper into the cave. I theorized to the camera about who could have made the carvings and why. Maybe they were gifts the Paiute Indians had made for the Wind Roller. As I talked, Fisher keep pausing me. He was having trouble getting the sound right against the wobbly echo of the cave, but he was skilled and quickly got us back on track, shooting me a thumbs up to continue.

We had to step carefully, because there were holes in the ground; some were as small as a teaspoon, most were the size of baseball gloves, and there were even a few as big as a twin beds. The holes were spread out and irregular. These definitely weren't natural formations.

And then we came across a chamber with something none of us truly expected to find; the massive exoskeleton of the Wind Roller. It looked like a dragonfly, only this was about a thousand times bigger. Its thorax was as big as a sports car with wings as long as a city bus drawn back along its body. The light from Salak's camera made the wings glow like cathedral glass. Its eyes were dark, hollow sockets. But the thing that caught my attention was a fifteen-inch-long clay cylinder in its mouth held in place by two curved pinchers.

Salak recorded the ancient creature from every angle. There were more of the clay cylinders scattered around the dragon's body. Some were tiny, no bigger than bullet casings with the same tiny grooves. Then I realized that the Wind Roller was the one that made the clay carvings. As big as the Wind Roller was, it was still too small to have made the ones at the entrance to the cave and too big to have made the tiny ones. Maybe it made the smaller ones in its youth, and never grew to its full potential to make the larger ones.

The cylinders looked like the old phonograph cylinders invented by Thomas Edison, long before the flat records or tape or anything digital even existed. I kept looking at the cylinder in its mouth. It probably dug up the raw clay from the floor and held it between its pincers and spun it. Maybe it breathed fire or extremely hot wind to bake it. But the question of why the Wind Roller made these cylinders remained a mystery.

There was something about the one in the Wind Roller's mouth that drew me to it. I stood in front of the dead beast, reached up, and spun the cylinder in its mouth. It let out a light whistle that echoed through the cave. I quickly stopped the spinning. For a second, I thought the sound was coming from the dead dragon, but then I realized whistling came from the pincer scratching against the clay. These were the dragon's audio recordings when it made the wind. Each new wind was a new song. Maybe these were like whale songs.

I spun the cylinder again, but faster this time. The whistling sound started to heat up, like a hot kettle starting to announce itself. I spun it faster and faster. The sound bounced off the walls. Fisher tried to adjust the sound before violently ripping his headphones away. He was the first to hear what was coming. The cylinders by our feet began to vibrate, rattle and jump. I turned to Salak and Fisher. It looked like they were calling out to me, but I couldn't hear them over the whistling.

But even when I stopped the spinning the sound never stopped. It actually seemed like it was coming from deeper in the cave and getting louder. This sound was chirpy and excited. The whistling became so strong, it felt like we were getting pushed out by a wave of sound. I didn't realize just how strong the sound was until we got disoriented and tripped into the holes. The malformed stalactites overhead started to fracture and fall down around us. The high pitch emanating from the darkness was getting louder. I was panicking, but couldn't afford to stop moving. We reached the bulky stalagmites. We had taken our time getting around them when we went into the cave, but now we were in a rush trying to navigate around these blockades.

I was the first to make it out past the mouth of the cave and back onto the open world. The sky was a blindingly bright shade of gray. The clouds moved quickly overhead, the grass rustled violently, and a small dust storm tore across the desert below. I turned back around to my crew. I waved and shouted for them to hurry. Salak and Fisher were close to the exit. Then I saw the swarm of tiny Wind Rollers closing in on them. It was then that I realized that the smaller recordings were from the dragon's children and I had just played their parents voice. They had just heard something they hadn't heard in decades, possibly centuries, and now they were hyperventilating at their mother's return. They were coming to find her and wouldn't stop searching until they did. I tried to get a good look at the creatures, but the sound coming from them was so loud that even my vision blurred. All I saw was a colorful flash of wings and jagged, biting pincers. And then there was a loud pop and all tones faded away, replaced by an all-consuming silence.

The whole mountain shook so violently that the long maw of the cave collapsed in front of me and my friends disappeared in the darkness. The wind stopped blowing. The clouds hung in place. The grass stopped rustling. I tore at the grass curtain and pounded and scraped at the rock, but it was too much for me to move on my own.

I rushed down the mountain to get help. I thought I'd tell them what I saw, but by time I got to the base, I realized it would be best not to go in saying that my friends and I were attacked by dragons, or else they'd think I was insane. When I found a ranger station, I wrote on a scrap piece of paper that I had gone deaf and my friends were trapped in a cave.

As our rescue team made the ascent, I wanted to tell them about the Wind Rollers, but who would ever believe me without proof? And all the evidence I had was trapped with Salak and Fisher. Our rescue team searched for hours, but we could never find the entrance to the cave again, and I was eventually told they had to give up the search.

It's been more than twenty years since that day I lost my hearing and my friends, but someday I'll find that cave and the Wild Rollers, the whole hive of them. I go back to Steens Mountain often to look for them. At first it was every day, then every month, and now it's at least once or twice a year. But each search always ends the same way: with me descending the mountain alone toward the motionless desert, out of breath and silent.

SCALE FOR GOLD

BY JAMES JAKINS

JULIA NEEDS A FIX. It's just been one of those days. Her boss was found dead in an old church early this morning. Magic overdose, the cops tell her. "Levitated out of his mind," the less tactful of the pair says.

She is not really surprised at Professor Wilkins's death. The man was an addict. He'd spent his evenings in that shell of a holy house practicing new spells. Finding new ways to escape the reality of the world.

But just because she knew this was how the man would die, it doesn't lessen the impact of his death.

"We found him with eggshell in his hand and bird shit on his face," the cop continues.

She nods in understanding. A simple spell, but the high is powerful. They'd likely found ash in his other hand, the components of the spell that had been used up to make the egg hatch and let the man's mind control the bird that emerged ready to fly. It was easy to just not come back from that one.

Once the officers leave Julia remains seated at her desk outside Professor Wilkin's office. She has no idea what this means for her. She'll likely need to find a new job. It's not likely the university will keep their Magic Studies professor's assistant on the payroll when their Magic Studies professor is dead.

Maybe Professor Johnson needs an assistant? Will the man even continue working after his partner's death?

Her left hand begins to shake softly. She needs a fix.

She picks up her phone and sends the text: *I need something now. Have any?*

The reply is almost instant: *You know it. But I'm running low on the red stuff. Up for another trade?*

She lets out a relieved breath before sending her response: *Of course. I'll be there in 15.*

She double checks inside her purse to make sure she does indeed have what the man on the other end calls "the red stuff."

Nestled between her wallet and a tampon is the red scale. The size of her palm, it's small as dragon scales go, but its value is not measured in size or weight. Its value lies in the magical potential that lives within.

This particular scale is very valuable. It has very recently fallen from the breast of a living dragon. This scale holds more magic than any of the components her contact sells to the local mages and other addicts.

True to her word she arrives at her destination in fifteen minutes.

Another old church. Not the one her deceased boss used for his spells, but another.

Churches are no longer used for their intended purposes. Not since the world ended and the angels descended from the Silver City to try and fix what man had destroyed.

No one seeking eternal salvation goes to church anymore. Instead, they go to one of countless Silver City Embassies and file the appropriate paperwork.

This leaves the empty places of worship for other uses.

Julia pushes the doors open and is greeted by the smell of bird shit and unwashed bodies.

A row of pews lined up against the wall holds several men and women. They are all slouched in their seats, crushed eggs held in loose grips, above them flit tiny birds, chirping happily. The humans grin stupidly as they watch with blind eyes, uncaring when one of the birds stains their face.

One of the birds soars out a broken stained-glass window and the woman on the edge of the bench slumps further, eyes closing.

Julia pretends to not notice.

Other benches hold more people, not all lost in their spells—"levitated out of his mind," the cop says—and the occupants watch Julia.

Some of the men watch her with hungry eyes, devouring her form. Others ignore her. They know why she's here. There is only one reason any one comes here.

They come here to see Jeff.

He's waiting for her in the usual spot. On a padded chair on the raised stage where once a preacher would have warned of sin and avarice.

He is finishing a conversation with another customer.

The woman is thin, hair flat and dead. He hands her a small bag—inside is a pinch of black dirt, a twist of blond hair, and a vial of rat blood. "Midnight. Cast the spell at midnight," he reminds her.

The woman nods as she practically rips the plastic bag from Jeff's grip.

Julia steps aside and lets the woman pass as she rushes for the door.

"Hey, J." Jeff's smile is thin, like the rest of him.

Julia doesn't return the smile. "Do you have it?" She sits on one of the two folding chairs set up in front of him.

Jeff's thin smile spreads further across his slender face as he reaches into the bag at his side and pulls out a small vial.

Julia lets out a sigh of relief at the sight of the contents.

Jeff's long, bony fingers shake the vial and the golden powder within glitters invitingly.

"I still don't know what you and that mage of yours do with this stuff." Jeff holds out his empty hand, waiting for his payment.

"It doesn't matter," Julia says, pulling out the scale and placing it in his open hand.

"Whatever you say, J." He hands her the vial after a quick study of the scale.

She rises to leave but stops. "Wait." She turns back to him, eyes darting, hoping no one can hear the desperation in her voice. "Is it from the same source as last time?"

Jeff nods, not really paying attention to her anymore. "Yeah. Shaved it off the brick myself. Genuine paving stone from the Silver City. Heavenly gold J. Just the way you and your boss like it."

Her relieved breath is ragged. "Great. Thanks."

She turns without another word, vial clutched to her chest, and makes her way out of the church. She ignores the eyes that watch her. Ignores the dead woman that no one else seems to have noticed. Ignores the smell and the desperation.

She walks quickly to her car. Once behind the shield of metal and glass she holds the vial up and studies it. The dull gold dust rustles softly as she shakes it.

Her hand trembles as she tries to unseal the bottle. The small cork evades her grasp on the first few attempts.

Finally, with a pop, it's free and the smell of the gold hits her. She breathes in deep; a moan that borders sensual escapes unbidden.

She should wait. She knows she should wait. She should drive home, lock herself in her room and then use it. But today has not been a good day and she lacks the self-discipline to resist the pull.

"Just a little," she tells herself and the open vial. "Just enough to stop the shaking."

Somehow, she is able to listen and only pours a pinch of the rough powder on the back of her hand.

She has enough sense to offer a cursory inspection of the surrounding street. No one seems to be paying any attention.

The gold is rough and cuts as she inhales.

"Oh, God." She throws her head back against the seat. The pain and pleasure of the substance fill her. An electric thrill courses through her and she shivers from the joy of it.

The streets of the Silver City are paved with gold. It is the original gold. It is not just gold but the essence of gold. Nothing found on Earth can compare with it.

Julia doesn't know why she craves it. None of her kind do. The insatiable hunger they experience all their long lives. But this gold fills the hole. At least for a little while.

She straightens in her seat, trying to remain motionless as her body continues to quiver.

Finally, she exhales. A plume of clean, white smoke fills the car and she is forced to open the window to let it out.

Today is still a horrible day, but, for now, things are looking up.

She pours another pinch straight into her mouth and she chews as she starts her car and pulls onto the street.

THE DRAGON'S TEAR
BY BO HERNÖ

DOWN IN THE bottomless depths of the Mariana Trench off the coast of Japan—as near to the center of the earth as could be reached—a never-ending stream of falling debris rained down into the murky depths unseen by man, disturbing a forgotten creature that lay dormant for unknown aeons. The creature stirred as it was slowly showered in humanity's short-sighted folly—the remains of unending consumerism. It raised its head and set its myriad eyes upon the world above, a place it had long ignored, but would no more. It opened its maw, letting out a sonar scream, sending shock-waves that rocked the ocean above for miles around, toward unsuspecting shores.

Falling asleep at the local internet cafe while still wearing his virtual reality headset was nothing new to whiz kid Hayato Arakawa. Neither the staff nor the other regulars would try to wake him. Over time, the frequency of his plugged-in cyber-slumbers increased, until one day, he didn't come out of it.

Undisturbed for nearly two days, he slouched over the computer desk with his decked-out head flat on the worn-down keyboard. It wasn't until a receptionist returned to work and saw him in the exact same position as the day before that anyone took notice.

An ambulance was called, but Hayato was declared brain-dead before they threw his body on a stretcher like a sack of potatoes and rolled him out of there.

The event was taken as a bad omen by many of the more superstitious customers, and for some time people avoided the room where they had found the man's slumped form. Even the staff avoided the place until the manager threatened them with termination.

When the janitor finally stuck his head inside the room, he beheld more than the expected dust and debris. On the floor in the middle of the room, several of the stationary computers stood clustered together, with the keyboards, screens and other hardware radiating outward like the rays of the sun. The baffled janitor fetched the manager, who was quickly followed by the rest of the curious staff as well as a not-insignificant number of customers.

The unique display made for a puzzling sight, but since none had any idea as to who had moved the computers around to create this work of faux-modern art, the equipment was all just moved back into its appropriate spots, and the whole thing was written off as a practical joke. Day after day passed, and what everyone had thought was a one-time occurrence turned out to be anything but. Every time the room was left unattended, the computers were moved around at random, or so it appeared to the confused staff. But it wasn't just that room; soon it spread to every room with any electronic equipment left unobserved.

Administrators and technicians followed in turn, looking for the cause of the mystery, but each of them left with no more clues than the last. All the while, things kept getting progressively worse; rooms couldn't be left empty for more than a few minutes before things started moving around.

Eventually, it went so far that the place temporarily closed, and the manager decided to finally call a psychic investigator.

. . .

A few weeks after the original incident occurred, the psychic investigator arrived, and the manager of the establishment let him in. The large entrance hall was filled to the brim with stacks of electronic equipment on the floor. From stationary computers, to laptops and handhelds, screens and keyboards, even the cash register had joined the gigantic heap of electronics. The investigator observed that in each and every room, except for a thin layer of dust, everything else looked pristine. Desks stood in their booths, half-filled drinks standing undisturbed where they had been left the day the cafe had closed. The same went for all the other furniture.

The investigator was just about to speak when they both noticed a sound like metal grinding on metal coming from the main hall. Running as fast as they could, they arrived to witness something heretofore unobserved. Whatever unseen force that moved the equipment now possessed the courage to operate in full sight of the two observers. Slowly at first, the mound of hardware and scrap reformed itself into ever-changing mechanical configurations.

Before long the desktop computer cases all connected to each other, bound together with a variety of cables and wires into a long, segmented, worm-like shape. The laptops and keyboards cluttering the floor followed suit, forming leg-like appendages at multiple points along the massive, writhing form. Following the length of the main body, computer mice and headsets attached themselves on the top, forming a flaring spine. The flat-screens clustered together around a ball of miscellaneous electronics to form the rough shape of an elongated head, glistening, in contrast to the silver and black frame, with every color known to man. A great bushy bouquet of wires formed at the end of the long tail. Likewise, a magnificent mane of cables sprouted around its head.

The manager and the investigator both froze as the mechanical creature turned its shining head their way. One of the screens that comprised its face flashed a video clip of a human eye.

It winked.

Faster than either of the two people could react; the mechanical beast slithered out the front entrance; no trace of it was left in the near-empty room other than some tracks in the dust and a slight swirl in the air. The two witnesses stood there in disbelief for some time before returning to the gray reality that had momentarily slipped them by.

Outside, rush hour was in full progress. Cars polished to a mirror shine honked their horns at each other and road-raging drivers shook their fists out their rolled-down windows. Multi-colored masses like indistinct blobs made of business suits, sweatpants, and hoodies moved along the side-walks in a steady, never-ending stream.

As the mechanical being burst forth from the gates of the

cybercafe and into the crowded streets, every head swerved towards it and eyeballs popped out of their sockets when seeing the strange apparition. The few cars that had managed to start moving in the slow sludge of traffic crashed immediately upon gaining sight of the beast rushing past them, increasing speed as it took aim towards the sky and shot off into the air. The computer creature snaked its way up through the space between the highrise buildings, exerting a mysterious magnetic pull on the environment. Metal plates tore from the walls and added a layer of scale-like armor along the creature's long body. Signs snapped away from storefronts and rose into the air, seeking the newly-formed being until their flickering neon tubes and blinking diodes illuminated the length of its snake-like body.

The letters on a huge neon sign ripped in pieces and reformed into the shape of two slender horns upon its head. Two rainbow diode strips attached themselves to its snout and hung down like thin, flowing mustaches.

The creature, now fully formed, glowed with so many lights as if it had absorbed a golden sun.

The stunned people standing out on the streets, gathered on balconies, and hanging out of windows all looked up at the golden dragon as it took flight up over the buildings, cutting through clouds and circling the entire city in a humongous figure eight.

A thundering rumble shattered the attention of the onlookers, it came from the direction of the harbor and shook half the city to the core. People were falling over themselves from the shaking ground as the thundering grew louder and an all-encompassing shadow blotted out the sun. Attention seeking parasites hunting the perfect selfie were crushed like ants below the stampeding mass of water from the tsunami wave as it crashed down the streets, plowing through anything in its path. Many more scrambled on top of cars and buses, floating away with the city's debris consisting of human-made trash and human trash alike.

The newborn dragon flew with haste in the direction the sound came from and saw the distant harbor by the horizon as a massive monstrosity slowly rose out of the salty waters of the city's bay.

A grotesque centaur-like crustacean with the elongated tail like the body of a green lobster with dozens of spindly millipede-like legs running down its sides. Its scaly upper body carried two massive rubbery arms with enormous claws like scissors made of chainsaws, large enough to slice cars in half. Its face was an enraged mass of globular eyes with a mouth filled with sharp snaggle-teeth that peeked out from between every eye in a mind-boggling fashion.

Using its many legs, the horrible underwater abomination scrambled onto the concrete shore, roaring into the shattered skies above.

It was hungry.

It was mad.

Mad hungry!

.   .   .

It had lived for long aeons below the waves, feeding on the transparent marine life of the sea bottom. But as fish had dwindled in number while the onslaught of artificial objects, shipwrecks, garbage, and powerlines had increased, it had developed a newfound appetite.

An appetite for the semi-modern wonder of electronics.

The shore was spotted like a sickly dalmatian with the wrecks of ships and boats that had been ripped open from fore to stern, split in half, savagely crushed in the monster's attempts to devour its precious cargo and steering equipment.

It grabbed an overturned truck with one of its claws, crushing it like a beer can before its impossible maw opened and swallowed it whole. Nothing seemed enough to satisfy the furious hunger that raged inside the monster.

Swooping from the sky, the golden dragon's glowing form slammed headfirst into the ravenous undersea dweller. The two of them crashed over the harbor edge and into the chilly water. The crustacean caught the dragon between its claws and gripped it tightly. The ancient being spun with surprising speed and let the dragon fly back across the harbor, where it smashed into a broken-down warehouse filled with smelly old fish, breaking it into several sparkling pieces.

• • •

The crustacean violently climbed back up onto dry land, ripping large chunks from the concrete piers in its maddened scramble to reach the golden dragon and finish it off. But by the time the horror reached the ware-house, the computers and other scrap metal had mostly reformed into the mechanical dragon's former glory.

The few survivors remaining around the harbor all prayed for good to prevail.

The dragon, now flashing with broken neon lights and sparkling electronics, dove straight towards the rubbery monster's face, ramming them both through the wall and into the concrete fields of the harbor. The warehouse finally crumbled behind them in a great cloud of debris.

The dragon flew in a circle and made a second dive for the crustacean monster. Right before it collided with the sea creature, the hideous beast split apart down the middle of its torso, revealing multiple rows of sharp teeth lining the inside of its thick neck and body as its tooth-filled eye-stalks flared out in a ripping and tearing cloud of chaos. The monster used the two halves of its torso as a set of giant jaws and snapped them shut on the now not so golden dragon's head, a move that would have decapitated a lesser being. The metal creature struggled against its bite, but as its head was slowly crushed, the dragon tried one last desperate time to attack the beast from below the waves. It wrapped its long, flashing, sparkling body around its enemy's, and slowly tightened until a loud crack echoed out across the harbor.

The entwined creatures stumbled and fell into the ocean where they landed on a half-consumed oil tanker, which ignited from the dragon's electric sparks and exploded both hero and villain.

On the shore stood a boy choir, singing a hymn to the fallen as they got splattered with bits of gore and computer wires raining from above. The Self-Defense Forces fired its cannons in a 100-gun salute, and in the darkening sky, a new star was born. It would forever be known as the dragon's tear.

FIN CHECK

BY CHRISTINE MORGAN

I DON'T KNOW why I still do it, but I always do. Any time I'm passing a sizable body of water, whether it's the ocean, a lake, a man-made reservoir, a wide river ... I always, always do.

Fin check.

Fin check, head check, tail check. Scanning for some shape to break the surface. A rising triangular fin or tapered head upon a sinuous neck, a bump with spouting blowhole, the flat paddle of a tail, the ominous moving-bulge wake of something big.

As a kid, I was fascinated by stories of lakes and lake monsters, leftover dinosaurs, legendary denizens of the deep. Each year when family discussion came 'round of where to take our summer vacation, some such lake or another was unfailingly my enthusiastic vote.

A vote no one else ever seconded, of course. Not when there were theme parks; was I crazy? Who wanted to be stuck in the foggy cold by some murky lake when there were roller coasters and thrill rides and snack bars and souvenir stands and girls in short-shorts?

Once, I tried to be clever, suggesting a trip to Hawaii. Golden sandy beaches, surfing, hang-gliding, volcanoes, hula dancers, luaus. My plan then, also, being to wheedle in a whale-watching excursion or glass-bottom boat … but, no … Hawaii was too expensive. And if Hawaii was too expensive, that Atlantis place was out of the question.

Other times, I'd angle for going on a cruise, Alaska or Mexico or the Caribbean maybe, and still get the same answer. I started to wonder why our parents even asked. Why open it up for discussion if they already had a limited selection of driving-distance destinations picked out? To let us think we had any actual power?

So, yeah, summer after summer, it was road-trips, fast-food, and motels. I'd spend the long hours in the car, mashed into a corner by my brothers, peering out the window whenever blue water glimmered. Hoping to see … something, anything … different and special. It didn't have to be the whole dang Loch Ness Monster or a ginormous killer prehistoric shark. Just … something.

What I mostly saw was speedboats and jet-skis. Yet I never got over the habit of looking. Habit? Habit, nothing. Urge. Compulsion. Obsession. Whatever it is, I haven't gotten over it. Still haven't to this day.

You might think that, being an adult now and in charge of my own destiny, I could have finally up and gone to all those places. You'd think I could have gazed at lakes and oceans to my heart's content.

Well, it turns out being an adult sucks.

I have no idea how our parents swung a two-week vacation every year, though I could finally understand, if not necessarily appreciate, the "oh that'd be much too expensive" reply.

There's also time off to consider, not to mention various hassles and logistics. There are spouses afraid of flying and kids with allergies, and what about the dogs, we'll have to kennel the dogs. Besides, the garage needs cleaning out … there's yardwork to be done … and we've been talking about fixing the porch roof …

And this and that and the other thing, until it really is easier to just stay the hell home.

My job does keep me on the road a lot, though not in any romantic rambling cross-country kind of way. It's back and forth and here and there around the metro area. Traffic and tolls. Coffee in a travel mug. Lunch usually drive-thru and scarfed behind the wheel.

But, we have a lot of rivers. Waterfront parks and riverfront drives. Bridges, a multitude of bridges ranging from eight-lane concrete interstate to delicate-looking suspension. A lot of rivers, a lot of water. A fair amount of shipping in the industrial district. A fair amount of recreational and pleasure crafts where it's more scenic. Some where the surface is flat and glassy-smooth, mirroring skyscrapers and clouds. Some where turbulence rushes whitewater between rocks and rock-edged pools.

Know what I do?

That's right. I fin check. Every time.

What all have I seen so far? Pretty much zilch. Occasional sea lions or otters down by the marina. Once, a giddy moment of *at last!* life-affirming excitement as water swelled up around a surfacing mass … that turned out to be engineering students from a local university testing their remote-operated submersible … I got in a damn fender-bender over that one, rear-ending the car in front of me.

I tell myself to knock it off, to just give up. There's never going to be anything, no incredible jawdropping sightings. No immense white whale or toothy plesiosaur is going to rise up and stun the world. No giant squid is going to snare and tear down bridges with writhing tentacles.

And yet … and yet … and yet …

Still. Fin Check. Every time.

Even now, especially now, as I'm sitting in bumper-to-bumper rush hour complicated by construction. I cast my gaze past joggers on the lakeshore path, moms with strollers, guys with dogs, kids on bikes. A few people are out in those stupid-looking pedal-boats. Ducks and geese that had been bobbing serenely take sudden flight in quack-honk cacophony, wings beating, shedding feathers and showers of droppings –

– because –

I stomp the brakes. The car behind hits mine, but we'd barely been moving and the impact barely registers. I'm unbuckled and out my door before the other driver even starts swearing at me.

– because –

Fin check and my god there's no mistaking, that *is* a fin for sure!

Rising eight feet above the surface, maybe ten, slicing water into sluicing wakes to either side. A fin, dark greenish-grey and mottled, somehow ridged, and spiny. With the swelling displacement of a huge long body … with a spine-crested head emerging … eyes the size of basket-balls, in soulless evil oil-black … gaping jaws and monstrous teeth …

It chomps one of the pedal-boats into bloodied shreds of fiberglass and flesh.

And, in the screaming chaos that ensues, I can only cheer.